More Praise for John Lanchester and *Reality and Other Stories*

"Triumphantly achieved . . . [restores] a due sense of eeriness to our current reality." —James Walton, *New York Review of Books*

"The eight tales . . . are meant to entertain, to take you out of yourself for a space—and that they deftly do."
—Maureen Corrigan, *Fresh Air*, NPR

"Very clever, very modern 'entertainments.'"
—Catherine Taylor, *Financial Times* (UK)

"A mind-bending collection about the multifaceted scariness of the way we live now."
—Alison Kelly, *Times Literary Supplement* (UK)

"[John Lanchester] is a versatile writer with a gift for making sense of the modern world."
—Susannah Butter, *Evening Standard* (UK)

"Lanchester has struck just the right balance. . . . By approaching the subject with clear plots and a well-defined style, he puts a strong and distinctive stamp on the murky pitfalls of technology."         —Lydia Bunt, *Arts Desk* (UK)

"All of John Lanchester's work is of a piece—he wants his readers to see our moment better, and then do something about it."
—Kim Stanley Robinson, author of the Mars trilogy

T0018510

## ALSO BY JOHN LANCHESTER

### FICTION

*The Wall*

*Capital*

*Mr. Phillips*

*Fragrant Harbor*

*The Debt to Pleasure*


### NONFICTION

*How to Speak Money*

*What We Talk About When We Talk About the Tube*

*I.O.U.*

· *Family Romance*

# REALITY

## AND OTHER STORIES

# John Lanchester

**W. W. NORTON & COMPANY**
*Independent Publishers Since 1923*

For information about permission to reproduce selections from this book, write to Permissions, W. W. Norton & Company, Inc., 500 Fifth Avenue, New York, NY 10110

For information about special discounts for bulk purchases, please contact W. W. Norton Special Sales at specialsales@wwnorton.com or 800-233-4830

Manufacturing by Lakeside Book Company
Production manager: Julia Druskin

Library of Congress Cataloging-in-Publication Data

Names: Lanchester, John, author.
Title: Reality and other stories / John Lanchester.
Description: First American edition. | New York : W. W. Norton & Company, 2021.
Identifiers: LCCN 2020045117 | ISBN 9780393540918 (hardcover) |
ISBN 9780393540925 (epub)
Subjects: LCGFT: Short stories.
Classification: LCC PR6062.A4863 R43 2021 | DDC 823/.914—dc23
LC record available at https://lccn.loc.gov/2020045117

ISBN 978-1-324-02015-8 pbk.

W. W. Norton & Company, Inc., 500 Fifth Avenue, New York, N.Y. 10110
www.wwnorton.com

W. W. Norton & Company Ltd., 15 Carlisle Street, London W1D 3BS

1  2  3  4  5  6  7  8  9  0

*for Nicky and Con*

The graves stood tenantless and the sheeted dead
Did squeak and gibber in the Roman streets
—*Hamlet*


Ghosts talking to us all the time—but we think their
voices are our own thoughts.
—David Foster Wallace,
manuscript annotation to
'Good Old Neon'


The Conservatives received twice as much money last
year from the wills of deceased supporters than it did
from living members, new figures reveal.
—BBC News, 22 August 2018

# CONTENTS

# SIGNAL

I tried to give the children an etiquette lesson while we were waiting at King's Cross on December thirtieth.

'You aren't allowed to ask for the Wi-Fi password before you say hello,' I said. 'That's the main thing.'

'Uncle Mike won't care,' said Toby, who was nine.

'He's nice,' said Mia, who was seven.

'Both of those things are true,' I said. 'Uncle Mike is nice, and he wouldn't care, but this is a life lesson. It's just not what you do. You say hello, you chat for a bit, and then you ask for the Wi-Fi password. It's simply one of the rules.'

'Fear? That's the other guy's problem,' Toby said. We had recently let him stay up too late to watch *Trading Places*, and this line had made a profound impact.

Michael wasn't my oldest friend and he wasn't my closest friend, but he was older than any of the ones who were closer and closer than any of the ones who were older, so he had a special status, as part of the furniture of my life, the kind of friend who when you're asked how you met you have to think for a while to remember. What he certainly was, though, unequivocally and by a huge margin, was my richest friend. Michael was loaded, seriously and unambiguously loaded. He was the kind of rich that even other people who were rich considered rich. He had made the money himself. It was all the more impressive because Michael seemed barely to have noticed. His peers and friends and rivals and colleagues were all amazed by the fact that Mike was now some kind of gazillionaire, but it didn't seem to make much impression on Michael himself. He'd drifted through Cambridge doing something scientific—engineering or maths, I think it was. I'd always thought that, like me, he was going to be an academic, but Michael had got a first and then stumbled into the City, and then shuffled or ambled through an escalating series of jobs in finance before 'going off to try something a bit different,' and it was at that point that it became clear he had ascended to some new stratosphere of international wealth. The first sign was when he invited us to join him on holiday for a week, and that turned out to mean a helicopter pickup in Battersea taking us to a private jet at Northolt, taking us to a yacht the size of a municipal tennis facility, and a week's cruising in the Med. And still it was never clear how Michael had done what he'd done. This was a characteristic that had been salient from the time we first met, at university: his ambient, all-purpose, omnidirectional vagueness. It was a well-meaning vagueness, but it could also be highly irritating, and there were certain situations in which it more or less guaranteed disaster, such as anything involving social life.

This was shaping up to be another of those occasions. Michael had 'bought a little place,' as he put it, which after he mentioned the address, and I did a certain amount of cyberstalking, turned out to mean an estate of several thousand acres in North Yorkshire. The previous owner had suddenly died and the estate had been sold, in the flattering and far from accurate language of the only newspaper report, to a 'mystery financier.' Michael had invited us to go up for New Year's Eve about a month earlier. Kate and I couldn't resist, despite knowing that, while the setting was guaranteed to be amazing, from the social point of view it was likely to be chaotic, or hard work, or both. On the other hand, we knew that halfway through the alleged holidays we'd be hallucinating with fatigue, and three days with someone else looking after our lovely but exhausting little ones would feel like the kind of thing that should be available on the National Health Service.

The trip up north felt like punishment for our hubristic attempt to change holiday routine. King's Cross was a maelstrom. The stress was magnified by the fact that Michael had said, by text, only that we'd be met at the station, without saying exactly where or by whom. Network Rail seemed to pride itself on displaying platform information at the last possible moment, so we were quivering like greyhounds as we waited to run to the train. Toby and Mia hadn't eaten and were holiday-cranky, and were demanding a trip to the Harry Potter Shop and to Platform 9¾. We didn't know what we'd be doing at the house, or how fancy it would be, and as a result had overpacked. It was a perfect storm of travel stress and bad omens. Kate looked at me.

'This is a look of mute reproach,' she said.

'Yep,' I said. 'Sorry. We'll wait for the platform info, get to our seats, and hope it sorts itself out at the other end.'

'Unless he just forgot.'

'No, he never forgets,' I said, which was true: Michael might mis- or disorganise things, but he never plain forgot them.

The rest of the journey was both better and worse than I had expected. There were as many people standing as sitting, and when I say standing I mean lurching, swaying, listening to music at the perfect volume to irritate everyone within a five-metre radius. Add to that overheating, an unexplained twenty-minute delay after Peterborough, and two motion-sickness-prone children. We got off at York and, in the general mayhem, Kate found a driver carrying a sign with a misspelled version of our surname. The subsequent ninety-minute car trip through the Yorkshire dark, stopping only twice, for children's pee and vomit breaks, was a week at Jumeirah Dubai by comparison.

The driveway of Michael's big house was so long that even after we got there it took a while to get there. The four of us came out of the cold into a double-height entrance hallway, to be greeted by no one at all, apart from a very, very tall man, at least six feet five, who was looking at his mobile phone as if he were struggling to get reception, and more interested in that than in any other form of human interaction. His response to a family of four bursting through the door was to do nothing except scowl at us, then drift towards the side hallway. The rudeness was compounded by an air of complete coldness and disconnection, as if he couldn't care less whether we lived or died.

'Hello,' Toby said. 'Very nice to meet you. My name is Toby. How do you do? Also, would you mind awfully telling me the Wi-Fi password?'

While Kate and I spluttered and glared at our firstborn, the man continued to walk away and vanished around the corner.

Silence settled in the entrance hall of the big house. There was a stag's head on the far wall. Large portraits of formally dressed people from previous centuries frowned from above the unlit fireplace. Presumably, they were ancestors of the previous owner. The unwelcoming, inhospitable, eerie quiet loomed and grew. It seemed, for a moment, as if we didn't really exist. It seemed, for a moment, as if coming here for the holiday had been a very bad idea indeed.

Then, as in a farce, from the other side of the hall came four members of the household staff in uniform; a smartly dressed couple in early middle age arguing heatedly in French; and our host, who was carrying a pair of roller skates and a copy of a book called *Option Volatility & Pricing* by Sheldon Natenberg, thickly interleaved with Post-it notes.

'The four-fifteen,' Michael said. He hadn't forgotten that we were arriving, but he had forgotten that we would be arriving at that exact moment, so he was too distracted to greet us or smile or say hello. 'Pickup at, say, four-thirty,' he said to himself. 'Ninety minutes across the moors. A few extra minutes for other journey variables. Six-thirty.' He looked at his watch. 'Yes!' And then suddenly there was the sweet smile and the abrupt sense of warmth and intimacy, which was why, after all, people did love him. 'Yes!' he said and hugged Mia and then Toby and then Kate and me. He hugged like a natural non-toucher who had taken professional instruction in how to overcome his instincts and hug, and then found, greatly to his own surprise, that he liked it. Which, in fact, was what he was, and the reason I know is that I gave him the course 'I Hate Hugging: Overcoming Your Fear of Intimacy Through Touch' as a fortieth-birthday present.

After that, everything became better. I don't mean better

from the social point of view, because Michael still didn't know how to introduce people, and, that evening, as we tried to work out who was who, it became clear that he had done exactly what we suspected, and invited an essentially random group consisting of us, a large selection of work acquaintances who didn't know one another, plus a few people he'd barely met but had asked at the last minute.

It seemed that there were roughly two dozen of us. Even the numbers were unclear and seemed to fluctuate from meal to meal, and there was never any seating plan or organization or itinerary or sense that anyone had thought about how to make the whole thing work. Balancing that, making the whole event feel like a lovely escape from reality, was the wonderfulness of the house itself, and the lavishness with which it was run. The house looked big from the front, but we quickly realised that it was much bigger still, built like a ship with its narrow end facing the lawn and the drive. The bulk of the building stretched out backward and included, from a tired parent's point of view, every possible amenity you could think of. There was a video-game room, there was a retro-gaming room, there was a home cinema, there was a bouncy castle in a heated and covered area outdoors. There was a swimming pool, there was a multisize inventory of bicycles. There was a dedicated children's library, with books ascending in age range from the floor level upward.

Michael gave us the tour, in his habitual style ('Um—pinball machine').

'I've never seen so much stuff for kids—it's like a kids' hotel,' I said.

'Previous owner. Mad about them,' Michael said. 'I like it,

means I don't have to think about what kids want. I know that sounds a bit selfish, but you know what I mean.' I did.

'It's brilliant!' Kate whispered to me. She was right, it was brilliant. And that was the great thing about the house, the fact that it was so functional, so thought-through, that it seemed to be looking after you of its own accord. Also, a small but crucial detail, the Internet connections were very poor. There was broadband—I mean, it wasn't Tora Bora—but the walls were thick and the frame of the building had a metal component, which meant that the Wi-Fi was so erratic that it was the same as not working. There was next to no 3G or mobile data. That was luxurious, too—not for the few poor souls who were forced to roam the halls looking for mobile reception, but for us. I gave up on the Wi-Fi and gave up on checking my phone. It was a holiday in itself to feel so out of touch, so uncontactable.

As for the children, we could more or less leave them to it. The school holidays had been going on for two and a half weeks already, and we were drained and resourceless from endless days of full-contact parenting. Here, that wasn't an issue. We sat with them while they ate their supper and then left them to a Disneython in the children's TV room. Then I wrangled them off to bed, a little hyper from the excitement and novelty—I mean me as well as the children—but still manageable. I needed one of the staff to help me find our room, up two flights of stairs, down two corridors, round a corner and then back again, unexpectedly, after all that twisting and turning, at the front of the house, overlooking the drive. The kids' very big room had a connecting door to our enormous one. We did faces and teeth, a perfunctory lullaby, I adjusted the lights so that they were low enough for Toby and high enough for Mia, and then I was back downstairs for dinner.

Conversation with this roomful of strangers was easier after the second drink. As the prune-and-Armagnac soufflé was served, Toby came down, announcing that he was worried and couldn't sleep. He seemed more scared than usual for his mid-sleep waking, but then it was a very big, very strange, very unfamiliar house.

I took him up to bed. On the way, I complimented Toby on having managed to find the dining room. He said that one of the other guests, the tall man we'd seen looking for a mobile-phone signal in the entrance hallway, had shown him.

'He was on his mobile the whole time,' Toby said. 'It was a bit weird.'

Looking back, all I can say in my defence is that it would have been very inconvenient to pay more attention to my sudden sense of unease. Easier to keep my head down and concentrate on having a good time. I found my way to the bedrooms by turning left at a huge pot of poinsettias, and when Toby fell back onto his bed he was asleep by the second bounce.

The next day started well. The children got themselves up and after making a determined but mercifully short attempt to get us up, too, went off in search of breakfast—did I mention that there was something called a nursery, which was a separate children's dining room? We slept in until after nine, an extravagance of unprecedented dimensions. We were woken by the subliminal awareness that somewhere in this huge mansion somebody was cooking bacon.

There was a moment of incongruity when it turned out that, in the middle of all this lavishness, we couldn't open the curtains. They were soft and thick and hugely heavy, but there was no obvious pulley or cord to get them apart. The very definition of a First World problem: unopenable curtains. Luckily, just as I was about to give up, Toby and Mia returned from breakfast. Toby saw what I was doing and, trying to suppress his manifest sense of triumph, pressed a little button by the side of the bed. The curtains silently glided apart and we were looking out at a vista of lawn, oaks, and cloudy sky, down the driveway on which we'd arrived the day before. The lawns were pristine and stretched into the middle distance.

'I wish you'd been good at maths instead of English,' Kate said.

'How did you know how to do that, darling?' I asked Toby. I had already noticed that one of the defining features of the house was that there were gadgets everywhere. Preferably buttons. The previous owner had evidently been button-mad. Everything from the curtains in the home cinema (oh, yes, forgot to mention, there was a cinema) to the reclining mechanism on the seats in the spa (oh, yes, forgot to mention the spa) to the sliding door through to our dressing room (oh, yes, forgot to mention the dressing room) operated by buttons.

'The tall man told me,' said Toby. 'He knew how it works.' Again, I felt uneasy, and again I ignored it.

At breakfast, there was that same sense of two dozen strangers thrown together by an indifferent destiny, and I had the impression that people were present who hadn't been at dinner the night before, and vice versa. No matter: the luxury was what mattered, what counted, what felt real. Toby and Mia had already disappeared off elsewhere. People muttered in desultory conversations and flicked through newspapers. Towards the end of the meal, Michael stood up at one end of the table and tapped a knife against a glass.

'Um,' he said. I tried not to catch Kate's eye. 'There isn't really a plan. For the day. Sort of, um, do whatever you, um, feel like. I thought we might go sort of shooting, you know, pheasants, so I'm going to do that and any of you who'd like to, um, do that can come too, at eleven or so, and have some lunch and so on.'

So that's what we did. First, I went to find our host for a quiet word, which in a house this size was not straightforward. Eventually, I was steered by one of the staff to his office. Michael was sitting at a desk with *Option Volatility & Pricing* propped up in front of him, writing on a Post-it note.

'There's no futures market for onions,' he said. 'Gerald Ford had it banned when he was a congressman for Michigan. The Onion Futures Act was passed in 1958. It's the main reason onion prices are so volatile. Are you coming shooting?'

I said that I was.

'We have to bury some of them,' he said—then, seeing that I had no idea what he was talking about, went on: 'The pheasants. We shoot so many there's just no market. A market failure of a sort. Market for shooting but not for eating. So they get buried, plowed under by a tractor. I'm trying to find a way of giving them away. Strange thought, a food you literally can't give away. I forgot to ask: How was the trip up?'

'Fine,' I lied. Then I counted to five, a technique I often employed with Michael, since if I changed the subject too quickly it would end up taking even longer: his face would look like what a rebooting computer's face would look like, if it had one. *Four . . . five.*

'Michael,' I asked, 'just wondering, who is the tall man?'

'I thought I'd said,' Michael replied, visibly returning from his reveries about the international onion market and pheasant mass burial. 'Hector. He works for me. Well, sort of. He'd probably say he works "with" me. I've noticed that that's a thing now, people say they work "with" you, not "for" you. They must think it sounds . . .' He faded out again.

'Hector,' I said.

'Oh, yes, he's a data-mining person. Sort of, takes a haystack and digs out the needles.'

'I'd like to have a word with Hector,' I said. 'Also, do you know if he has kids? I know he hasn't got any kids here, but does he have kids in general?'

'Um . . . yes. By a previous marriage. They came on the yacht once. The ex-wife seemed to be extremely cross with him— you sort of wondered why they were married. They're with her this Christmas. Boy and a girl.' Michael got up and came round his desk.

I felt a sense of relief. Tall Hector was missing his children, so his interest in mine could easily be explained by that, and his wandering around semi-Aspergerishly on his phone when we'd first arrived would be accounted for by the kind of work he did: he was that type of person. Still, I felt that I should meet him. Michael took me on a tour of the public rooms (sitting room, library, salon, reading room, billiard room), and then we knocked on the door of Hector's suite, all without result.

'Probably gone for a walk. Some of them did. If he doesn't

come shooting, or we don't bump into him in the course of things, I'll introduce you at dinner.'

Toby and Mia didn't want to watch grown-ups shoot, so Kate gave the woman in charge of the house instructions not to let them out but to let them play video games or watch films or whatever until we got back. We headed off in a convoy of Land Rovers to an exposed patch of high ground a few miles away. I think slightly more than half our fellow-guests came. The beaters and drivers or whatever they're called were all in place. A reassuringly huge set of picnic baskets was arranged across trestle tables. Some of the party, who had clearly been forewarned, wore spectacularly complete English shooting drag, tweed waistcoats and jackets and caps and trousers and so on. A few of us, Kate and I very much included, were in jeans and trainers. The lugubrious man in charge of the shoot did not look impressed. He held out a bag and said, 'Draw a peg.' We did: I was No. 4, Kate No. 9. We set up with shotguns at our appointed spots. I introduced myself to the men on either side of me. One of them was a Hungarian former physicist who worked for Michael in some capacity that he either could not or would not explain, and who spoke what you'd have thought was an unemployably small amount of English. I don't know who the man on the other side of me was, because he didn't say anything. The pheasants were driven toward us, and we shot them, with varying degrees of competence. The argumentative Frenchwoman gave a small squeak every time her shotgun went off—and hit more pheasants than anyone else. I'd done this only once before, and set myself the target of hitting a single pheas-

ant, which eventually, some way into the second hour, I did.
While we were shooting, the clouds turned dark and threatened
rain, but it stayed dry.

Lunch was—perhaps a macabre touch, but I appreciated it—
pheasant sandwiches. Also caviar and blinis, cooked to order
on a spirit stove, salad of salsify and chopped egg, custard tart,
Billecart-Salmon rosé. The small talk continued to be hard
work, but the shooting made it easier, because if the person you
were talking to was hard going you could always point at the
sky, say *bang!*, mime a pheasant falling to earth, and hold up a
single finger. I did this with my Hungarian physicist. He looked
at me, nodded slowly, and held up four fingers. I thought, Yeah,
right. After lunch, we were given new pegs and shot some more
pheasants. I got another one.

Parental guilt, largely dormant while we were on the shoot,
began to kick in on the way back, but, when we got to the
house, a short unfrantic search found Toby and Mia parked in
front of a *Star Wars* film in the TV room. In order to keep the
level of digital distraction sufficiently intense, Toby had picked
up an iPad—not his, a house iPad—and was playing a side game
of *Plants vs. Zombies*.

'What did you have for lunch?' Kate asked.

'Beans,' they said in unison.

'Did you get bored?' I asked them as they sat side by side in
matching reclining chairs, their legs not reaching to the end of
the footrests.

'It's *Star Wars*,' Toby said, as if to a simpleton. 'We're on the
second one now.'

Kate and I exchanged a guilty look. We seemed to be doing
a lot of that. We were having a good time, but it would also be

possible to construct a case that we were the worst parents in the world.

'It was clever of you to get the new film and set up the screen and everything.'

'The tall man did it.'

Kate and I looked at each other. Hector was lonely and missing his children. It made sense. But then Kate noticed something, and that was when the holiday went irrecoverably wrong.

'Your hair is wet,' she said. 'You went for a swim?'

'Yup,' Toby said. 'The tall man took us.'

'The tall man went swimming with you.'

'Yes. No. He didn't get in. We went to the pool and wanted to go swimming, but there were no grown-ups there so we couldn't, but then the tall man came and he let us in because he could reach the lock thing and then he waited by the side while we swam and then he went away. He was on his phone the whole time. He's always on his phone.'

'The tall man was on his phone? Was he.' I tried to keep my voice level.

'Did he look like he was filming you?'

'Maybe. I dunno. Maybe not. He kept moving his phone about. Even when we were in the changing room he was waving the phone about.' I felt ill. I suddenly made a connection—the sight of Toby pressing the home button on the iPad was what did it.

'When the tall man told you how to make the curtains open in our bedroom, remember that? Pressing that button thingy? Did he just tell you, or did he come into the room and show you?' I knew what Toby was going to say.

'We were looking and couldn't find it, and he came in and

showed us. He was on his phone then, too, when he came in our room. He's always on his phone. He never says anything, he just keeps looking at his phone.'

I went at speed to look for Michael. I found him back in his office with his text-book. I told him we needed to find Hector, right away. He got up and came with me and we did the same circuit we had done earlier in the day. The house seemed to have refilled with guests during the afternoon, as people came back from whatever pursuits they'd been pursuing and started looking forward to dinner. Michael did a lot of smiling and nodding as we passed people in the corridors, the salon, the sitting room.

We found Hector in the library. A swarthy man with smooth dark hair was sitting in a red leather armchair with a copy of the *Financial Times* and a cup of tea. At a single glance, I could tell that he wasn't the man we had seen in the hallway when we first arrived.

'Hector!' Michael said. 'Can I introduce my old friend David?'

Hector bounced to his feet. He was, at a generous estimate, five feet seven. I took his hand so distractedly I can't have failed to seem rude. Then I said, 'Excuse me,' and dragged Michael out of the room.

'Michael, what the hell? I said the tall man. In fact, I said the very tall man. I was extremely specific. The whole point was how tall he is.'

Michael blinked at me. 'Hector is tall. Unusually so. He is Bolivian, and they are the second-shortest people in the world. Average male height is one-point-six metres, or five feet two. Hector is many centimetres taller than that. If he were Dutch and was that much taller than the national average he would be six feet eight. He could be a professional basketball player!'

I took a breath and wrestled for a moment with the desire to punch my close old friend in the face. *Three . . . four . . . five.*

'Okay, Michael, here's the thing. One of your guests has been behaving, let's just use that all-purpose word "inappropriately," with my children. Going into their room at night, taking them for a swim, coming into the children's room when they're watching a film. Okay? That clear enough for you? The person doing that is the tall guest. The one who is genuinely tall by any sane person's standards, not your bloody data person who could in some parallel universe be a Dutch basketball player if it weren't for the fact that in real life he's actually a fucking Bolivian dwarf.'

Michael sat completely still, usually a sign that he was thinking hard.

'Very tall,' he said.

'Jesus, Michael? How clear do you want it to be? Yes, very tall.'

He thought a bit more.

'No,' he eventually said.

'What do you mean, no?'

'There are no guests that could be reasonably described as very tall. Taking that to mean, significantly in excess of six feet. I'm not sure that you yourself aren't the tallest man here.'

That punch-old-friend-in-face feeling came back over me.

'Look: We saw him. When we arrived, he was right there in the hallway. In fact, we saw him before we saw you. A rude cold tall man. He went out just before you came in from the other side.'

'No,' Michael said again. 'I'm sorry, but that doesn't fit my recollection. You were alone when I came in—I mean, except for some of the house people who were there to show you to your room and whatnot.'

'Michael, I know social life and small talk and all that stuff aren't really your thing, but is it possible you have somebody here you don't know about? Somebody you accidentally invited in a casual moment and then forgot about? Copied in on an email by mistake? Had a few drinks, blurted out a New Year's invitation, and they took you up on it without your realising?'

'No,' he said, yet again. 'I'm sorry, but no. There is no possibility that there is a guest here I don't know about.'

We both fell silent. It was easy to imagine how somebody could be moving around the house without being fully identified, since we were all essentially strangers to one another. The fact that this somebody was not a guest was what I found most disturbing. This meant that there was a man roaming around who wasn't supposed to be here, and who was taking an unsolicited interest in a nine-year-old boy and a seven-year-old girl, especially when there were no adults around. Michael and I came to no conclusion, and I could tell he thought that we had not seen quite what I knew we'd seen when we arrived, and also that the children were exaggerating or lying or had got imaginatively stuck on an inaccurate description of somebody, probably a member of staff. To be fair to him, I might have thought the same thing, if I hadn't seen the tall man with my own eyes.

➤

That night was New Year's Eve. A big evening was planned, with dinner and then a huge bonfire, where we were supposed to gather to toast the arrival of January first. I decided to skip all of it. After talking to Michael, I went to see Kate and we decided that it was too late to leave, but we would not let the children out of our sight for the rest of the day. Kate sat with them while they ate their supper and then went to dress for dinner while I read them a story and got them settled. Then I took up position in an armchair opposite the doorway, turned off the light, and just sat there. It felt like an expiation, a penance for I don't quite know what. The leather chair squeaked when I moved, and the children murmured complaints for the first quarter of an hour, but once they'd fallen asleep I was free to wriggle about.

Time passed slowly. Although we were at the opposite end of the house and on the first floor, I could sense the big dinner party, the thrum and vibration of company and cooking and coming and going around a big crowded table. The bedroom was warm, and I alternated between feeling drowsy and anxiously, jerkily awake. Toby and Mia took turns muttering and shifting in their sleep. After a couple of hours, I could hear voices and movement; dinner had finished. Kate came into the room, pantomiming cat-burglarishly as she tiptoed in. She went through into our room, changed into many layers of warm clothing, came back to kiss the children once again, and headed off into Phase II of the celebrations. Noise came and went as doors opened and closed, and there were subtle drafts as guests went through the big doors at the front of the house. Then it grew properly quiet again. I sat and fidgeted and daydreamed, never managing to be either entirely comfortable or uncomfortable. I thought about the identity of the tall man. I thought about Michael and the ways in which he had and hadn't changed. I thought about the lectures I was giving next term, and how sick of them I was, and whether or not I could be bothered to write another course. I remembered back to the time I'd written these, in the first year of my first job, two decades ago, while Michael and I were sharing a flat, when nothing about the idea of being in my rich old friend's huge house with my two children asleep in the room, and my wife outside at a bonfire, would have seemed in any way imaginable. I thought about the ways in which I liked my life and the ways in which I was disappointed by it.

I may have fallen asleep. I'm not sure. What happened next was in the margin between dreams and full consciousness. I knew where I was and what I was doing, but my volition seemed to have been dialled down so that I could not move or speak. I saw the handle of the door, directly across from where I was sitting, start to move. It was easy to tell, because it was an irregular wooden handle and the pattern of light shifted on it as it turned. The door began, very gradually, to open. The figure in the doorway was backlit from the light in the hall, and I couldn't see its face, but I could see that it was a man. A tall man. Slowly and in complete silence, he came into the middle of the room. He was holding a phone in his right hand, and when he got to the middle of the room he lifted it up to his face. For the first time, I could see his eyes. In the reflected light of the phone, they were completely white. There was no pupil and no iris. I ordered myself to stand, but couldn't. I felt as if there were nothing left of me but a compound of fear and helplessness.

The man walked across to Toby's bed and stood over my sleeping son. He held the phone out over Toby and moved it up and down. He looked at the phone and shook his head. Then he crossed to Mia's side of the room. He held the phone out again. There was a faint murmur, as if he was whispering to himself. He kept looking down at the children and then back at his phone. He never looked at me. After standing by Mia's bed for what felt like a long time, he shook his head again and went back to the middle of the room. Then he bowed his head for a moment, as if in prayer or resignation, and walked out of the bedroom. The door closed smoothly and silently. There was no noise of footsteps, but there was a regular tapping noise that hadn't been there before. It took me a few seconds to realise that it was my heartbeat, and that I was now, if I hadn't previously been, fully awake. I got up and ran to the door and opened it. The corridor was empty. Through the window at the far end of the hallway, facing over the back of the house, I could see the distant flames of the New Year's celebratory bonfire. I ran to the window, from which the corridor forked left and right to the two wings of the house. There was nobody to be seen.

———▶———

We left before breakfast. There were no trains, so at six I texted Michael's driver, the one who'd picked us up, to ask if he would, as a private arrangement between him and me, take us all the way home. We agreed on a rate of a pound a mile, which at the time I felt was the best two hundred and fifty pounds I would ever spend. I would have said goodbye to Michael if I had seen him, but he wasn't up yet, so I didn't. We carried our own bags downstairs at seven o'clock, and the driver was waiting. He helped Kate and me shove our cases into the trunk.

The car set off down the long driveway. It had been cold overnight, and a hard frost had settled on the lawns and on the gravel, so the driver went slowly. When we got a few hundred yards from the house, my phone suddenly blossomed with texts and messages and missed calls. I took it out and looked: nothing important, just the electronic detritus of modern life. The driver laughed.

'That always happens,' he said. 'Used to drive the previous owner mad. Did everything he could to get reception inside, and none of it worked. He'd wander about the house, cursing the weak signal. He hated it, because he was mad about his gadgets. We used to say the two loves of his life were his gadgets and his children. And the sad thing was, that was how he died. He was driving up here, tried to send a text to say he was running late. Texting and driving—bad combination. Car turned over. When they cut him out of the car, phone was still in his hand.'

'Stop the car,' I said. We crunched to a halt. I found myself breathing heavily. I undid my seat belt and got out.

The grass was stiff with frost. I leaned down to my open door and said, 'The previous owner—was he a tall man?' but I didn't wait for an answer, because I knew what it would be. I stood and turned and looked back at the house. Standing at the window of the children's bedroom, a familiar shape appeared in silhouette. I couldn't see him clearly, but there was a sharp flash of light, and then another, and then another. I realised that the light was coming from something in his hands, moving from side to side, catching the early-morning sun and dazzling it back at us, as he turned and moved and shifted, always moving, always adjusting, forever straining for that elusive thing, forever seeking, trapped in a moment that would never end, trying to find a signal.

# COFFIN LIQUOR

## Monday

I realised that things had gone wrong as soon as I arrived at my hotel. The receptionists spoke no English. Only when I showed them my passport did they seem to accept, with reluctance, that I had a booking. I was given a key and took my own bag upstairs. The room was a cramped, over-furnished space with thin brown walls. On the desk was an envelope of conference materials including a lanyard and a printed programme. It was at that point that I realised I had been enticed to attend the event under a misleading prospectus. The first talk on the first morning was titled, 'What economists can learn from Vlad the Impaler: narrative, belief, and the immanence of the imperceptible.'

In short, I find I have been brought to this godforsaken country in Central Europe—I say godforsaken purely as a figure of speech—to attend a conference on the dialogue between economics and the humanities under entirely false pretences. My

views on this subject are well known. The conference organiser's, or purported organiser's, contact details were appended
to the covering letter. I rang his mobile immediately.

'Professor Watkins,' the man said, with the devilish nerve to
sound as if he were, of all things, amused. 'A pleasure to hear
from you. The flight was satisfactory? The hotel?'

I was polite but firm. 'You, sir, are an impostor. I bid you
good night.' I disconnected from the call and sat down to write
this journal. And now to bed. My hopes for the start of the conference tomorrow could not possibly be any lower.

## Tuesday

I slept poorly. The atmosphere of this room is oppressive. The
building creaks as it settles. The heating is set high and cannot
be turned down, and when I opened a window I was greeted by
intermittent carousing from the street outside. An uncomfortable night. Breakfast was dark bread and black jam. Not bad.
A number of other guests were eating the meal on their own; I
surmise that they too are conference attendees.

The conference centre is a short walk away from the hotel,
about four hundred metres. The medieval architecture of the
town is picturesque for those who have that taste, but not effi-
cient. The streets are narrow and winding and poorly adapted
for their contemporary mix of human and vehicular traffic.
Generations of superstition and feudal oppression followed by
a few decades of Communist rule followed by a belated transi-
tion to a full market economy have all left their mark. It is an
airless and gloomy town.

The conference venue is a box-like concrete building with

subtly flickering lighting and erratic currents of hot and cold. I
arrived promptly for the first plenary session. I shouldn't have
bothered. The conference has a 'dual chair,' and both of them
made introductory speeches. The first chair is an Italian macro-
economist of about my age. He spoke some sense about econo-
metrics but then veered off into some whiffle about dialogue
and conversation and paradigms. Overall, poor. He was suc-
ceeded by a female Eastern European literature professor in
early middle age who had hair with a blue streak in it and purple
glasses. Also bangles. There ensued a series of platitudes, false-
hoods, mischaracterisations, illiteracies—an entire thesaurus of
modern nonsense. The ostensible subject of her speech was the
continuing contemporary importance of myth, but from the
point of view of a properly trained mind—i.e., mine—there
was no content at all.

Attendees listened to the speeches by the means of simulta-
neous translation through earpieces. At the end of her talk it
was a pleasure to take mine out. Others around the hall were
doing the same, stretching and chatting and moving from their
seats. I did not sense the general atmosphere of mutinous dis-
approbation which would have been fitting. There was to be a
short break followed by smaller sessions in other rooms on specific sub-topics. My own talk, to a session on recent work on
supply-side policy, is not until Thursday. The idea of spending
the whole day trapped in this building listening to nonsense
was insupportable.

I left the conference building and stood in the square outside.
Since the day was now mine, I decided to take the opportunity
for a little sight-seeing. I had brought a guidebook and there
was a selection of places of interest within convenient walk-

ing distance of the hotel. The closest was a famous church and graveyard of both architectural and historical consequence. I took some refreshment at a café in a side street and wandered through the paved lanes towards my intended destination. This is the medieval part of the town. The buildings were close on either side; many of them had arcades for, according to the guidebook, the dual purposes of keeping off summer sun and winter rain. It would have made an excellent setting for a film. There were no perspectives or vistas, merely a constant sense of turning and altering one's orientation as one wove through the town. It came as a surprise when I turned a corner and found myself at the entrance to a graveyard. A decrepit stone arch, the equivalent of an English church's lych-gate but taller and more forbidding, opened onto an oblong patch of crammed, stacked graves. They were so densely pressed together that they seemed to be squeezing against each other, as only living things can. Some of them protruded sideways and upwards at erratic angles, like a mouthful of unstraightened teeth.

An old woman in a shawl sat on a chair by the entrance to the graveyard. She held out a small woven basket, clearly demanding money. A sign advertised the cost of admission. I handed over the trivial sum and in return took an informational leaflet. I skimmed it as I crossed the graveyard and began looking around the church. Some of it I already knew. The church had strong historic associations with a monstrous former feudal overlord of the town. The count had been a famous torturer, whose favourite practise was to exlinguate his victims (this being the leaflet's term for cutting out tongues, a neologism, I suspect), then partially dismember them, then bury them alive. In time the townspeople had risen up against him and he had been subjected to his own favourite treatment. After death he took his revenge through vampirism. He and a large number of his victims were buried in the graveyard.

It goes without saying that I was sceptical. I am familiar with the scientific explanation of this and similar narratives. A rash of deaths—their real cause inevitably viral or bacteriological— affects a place. Causes are sought, and found in the arenas of legend and superstition and dream. A panic begins. Since the living are victims, the perpetrators must be found among the dead. Exhumations occur. Some bodies are found to have characteristics indicating postmortem existence—for instance, hair and fingernails that appear to have grown. In other cases the liquefaction of improperly preserved corpses leads to the creation of the substance known as 'coffin liquor.' As a result, in some crypts, coffins appear to have moved or burst. Supernatural phenomena are credited as the cause. Fear and superstition triumphs over science, and myths are born.

I did not find the church's architecture to be distinctive. Or perhaps it is merely that the medieval world was so encrusted with superstition and fantasy that it holds little appeal for me in purely aesthetic terms. Once you have seen a single gargoyle, a single buttress, you have seen them all. The interior was murky and the windows small and high. It did not take me long to conclude I had done enough. The principal point of interest was a series of funerary inscriptions—or rather, the place where the inscriptions had once been. The words had been scratched out and all that remained was blurred indentations in the stone. According to the leaflet, these monuments all belonged to the family of the notorious count: descendants of his victims had sought to erase all trace of his and his family's existence.

I went back out into the graveyard. The day had clouded over, and the whole world was now black and grey. I went to the place where the count had been tortured, exlinguated, partially dismembered, and thrown into a pit. Lime had been thrown in after him and stones piled on top, and then earth on the stones. For centuries the grave had gone unmarked, but many generations later the site was given a small plaque with nothing other than his name and dates. The story was graphically told on the photocopied leaflet, which, though not free of superstition, was nonetheless preferable to being trapped in that conference listening to otiose humanities-based pseudo-scholarship. I had chosen better.

It was this thought which gave me my brilliant idea. I could choose not to be in the conference by not being there, but perhaps I could also choose to not be at the conference, even while I was there. I could go into a form of internal exile. The medium for doing so was simple: the translator's earpiece. One was supposed to plug these into a small radio device, not much larger than a box of matches, and listen to the approved feed of the conference. But there was nothing to stop one from plugging the earpiece into a different device, a smartphone, say, and instead of listening to sociological flummery about canon formation and the structure of myth, hear something interesting and intelligent.

An excellent plan. I took out my mobile and opened the relevant app. A number of audiobooks were on offer at a special price. My mood called for something not-modern, something substantial; if the conference was to be the epic waste of time it promised to be, I would at least come back with some happy memory to show for it. Winter. Dickens. Yes. My finger hovered for a moment over *A Christmas Carol*, but although this would have been seasonally appropriate, I dislike the supernatural apparatus of that particular tale.

So no Christmas nonsense for me. I settled instead on *Great Expectations*, a book I have not read for a number of decades. I began the download. At this point, an unwelcome intervention occurred. The old woman from the entrance had, without my noticing, come towards me while I was looking at my phone, and was now standing in front of me, bent-backed and gasping with effort, waving the stick on which she had been leaning.

'Rău!' she said, shouting, pointing at my phone and then at the grave. 'Rău, rău, rău!'

The implication was that she was objecting to my using my mobile at that particular site. I decided to make light of the situation.

'Nothing wrong with my data plan, madam!' I said. 'It's covered under my UK allowance!' Which in fact happened to be true. If it had been otherwise I would have waited until I was on Wi-Fi before downloading the book. One can run up very substantial bills otherwise. But my levity did nothing to appease the hag.

'Rău, rău!' she kept shouting. And then, stretching for what little English she knew, 'No! Very bad!'

I am always polite and reasonable, even when provoked.

'You are a silly, silly woman,' I said to her. 'Go away.' My words had no effect. The download completed as I left the graveyard and the crone in my wake. I have returned to the hotel to write up this diary and may attend some of the conference this afternoon, now that I know I have the means of intellectual escape.

## Wednesday

The day began with a small but nonetheless piquant disappointment. In the morning, rather than be sucked into any breakfast small talk, I decided to make a start on the Dickens.

As I have already said, the fact that this story has no obtuse supernatural component was one of my reasons for downloading it. It was therefore with consternation that, on starting the app, I found my recollection to be inaccurate. Anyone who has read the passage where Pip encounters Magwitch in the graveyard for the first time will remember it, but there were aspects that I had not accurately recalled. The passage concerned was when Magwitch leaves Pip.

At the same time, he hugged his shuddering body in both his arms—clasping himself, as if to hold himself together—and limped towards the low church wall. As I saw him go, picking his way among the nettles, and among the brambles that bound the green mounds, he looked in my young eyes as if he were eluding the hands of the dead people, stretching up cautiously out of their graves, to get a twist upon his ankle and pull him in.

When he came to the low church wall, he got over it, like a man whose legs were numbed and stiff, and then turned round to look for me. When I saw him turning, I set my face towards home, and made the best use of my legs. But presently I looked over my shoulder, and saw him going on again towards the river, still hugging himself in both arms, and picking his way with his sore feet among the great stones dropped into the marshes here and there, for stepping-places when the rains were heavy or the tide was in. To my horror, I saw that the graves behind him were indeed unquiet. A form which resembled half a person was dragging itself out of the ground. The figure crawled not in the direction of the departed man, but towards me. It saw me look at it and stretched out its arms and made a wordless noise, which carried to me on the salt breeze. I turned again and ran until my legs could carry me no further.

I had forgotten that the afternoon part of the conference included a choice of excursions. This was more satisfactory than being subjected to the boredom and time-wasting of the main sessions, so I allowed myself to join in a group going on a tour of the main art gallery. One of the art historians at the conference conducted the tour. He was a satisfactory guide on questions of history and technique, less so when the discussion turned to more speculative matters.

The gallery is housed in the former castle, half of which is now given over to town offices. It is a picturesque building with turrets. The quality of the pictures was surprisingly high. This country had a few well-known artists from the Renaissance and a number of modernist painters of international reputation, who collected the work of each other and their contemporaries, and as a result the collection was bigger and better than I had expected. The tour took about two hours. We sat in a nearby café afterwards, a table of perhaps eight of us. One of the group, an art historian but not the one who had conducted the tour, asked me what I thought of it.

'Interesting,' I said, 'informative. I confess I did not know that our hosts had the cultural resources that they evidently do.' And then, because candour is an intellectual duty, I went on: 'Of course, I cannot help regretting the essential waste of energy involved.'

My interlocutor seemed surprised and asked me to clarify my remark.

'I mean, the waste of energy involved in the choice of subject for the pictures. The waste involved in painting pictures of things that are not true.'

Unless I was imagining things, she had the air of thinking that this was funny.

'So the Dürer crucifixion, for instance, which our colleague was arguing for as the highlight of the collection—your main conclusion about that is not to do with the emotional power, the question of realism versus theatricality as we discussed it earlier, the tension between the physical agony and spiritual transcendence, even the contrast between the picture and the frame, the questions of material culture involved—none of those things, but just, it isn't true?' she said, smiling.

'Correct. I would be failing in intellectual honesty if I did not point out that some of the words you use have no meaning, but I accept the many aesthetic virtues of the work. My point is merely that it is a shame that Dürer lived in a time when he had no choice—and incidentally I accept that he had no such choice and that this is not an act of will or inattention on his part, it is a tragic consequence of living in a benighted age—he had no choice except to squander his talent on myths and legends and fantasies and, to put it bluntly, other nonsense. If he had a subject of greater truth and consequence, his painting would have been better. Your next rhetorical device will be to ask me if I can supply an example of such a subject, so I will spare you the effort. He could have painted a great picture about the difference between mitosis and meiosis, or how photosynthesis works, or Boyle's law, which should be of interest to you, madam, since it applies to hot air. Now I give you good day.' And with that I left the café and went back to my room.

Against stupidity the gods themselves contend in vain. It made a dispiriting end to the day. I turned out my light and slept fitfully. The hotel was as noisy and unsettled as it had been on previous nights.

## Thursday

Since my session at the conference is this afternoon, I felt it was in accordance with norms to attend the entire day of talks and discussions, despite the fact that most of the talks would be annoying and stupid and I would be certain not to learn anything. I would not say that I was glad I did but norms of behaviour are important and the apparatus of conferences and scholarship is a valid thing, even if many of the things said and done at them are not.

Besides, although I did not have great expectations, I had *Great Expectations.*

The morning was divided into two parts. I had a choice between panel sessions on a range of unappealing topics and in the end went into one at random. This was a mistake, since the session turned out to be called 'Ghosts, Werewolves, GDP, and other Unknowables.' A behavioural economist gave a short introduction to recent developments in nudge theory, and then some literary scholars and anthropologists started in on their tripe. I discreetly—norms!—unplugged my earpiece from the radio which was carrying the translation and plugged it instead into my mobile phone. I started the app and was soon back with Pip in his unfortunate childhood on the Kent marshes.

I once or twice took the opportunity to check in on the translation feed.

'. . . which is why the issue of liminality, as expressed in the mythopoesis of the supernatural, can be said to figure . . .'

I had now got as far as the visit to Miss Havisham, one of my favourite passages in the book. Dickens's knowledge of the processes of ageing and dementia was, obviously, not scientifically modern, but to a surprising extent he still had an evidentiary basis for some of his fictionalised account. Cf the narcoleptic fat boy in the *Pickwick Papers*. Obviously a fully modern knowledge of these areas of medical science would have made Dickens a better and more complete writer.

Pip had made his visit to Miss Havisham and was leaving her premises after being frightened by Estella's cruel game with an effigy. It had woken superstitious feelings in him, which Dickens, if my memory served (it usually does), cleverly renders vivid without endorsing any nonsense of their supernatural origin.

Nothing less than the frosty light of the cheerful sky, the sight of people passing beyond the bars of the court-yard gate, and the reviving influence of the rest of the bread and meat and beer, would have brought me round. Even with those aids, I might not have come to myself as soon as I did, but that I saw Estella approaching with the keys, to let me out. She would have some fair reason for looking down upon me, I thought, if she saw me frightened; and she would have no fair reason.

She gave me a triumphant glance in passing me, as if she rejoiced that my hands were so coarse and my boots were so thick, and she opened the gate, and stood holding it. I was passing out without looking at her, when she touched me with a taunting hand.

'Why don't you cry?'

'Because I don't want to.'

'You do,' said she. 'You have been crying till you are half blind, and you are near crying again now.'

She laughed contemptuously, pushed me out, and locked the gate upon me. I went straight to Mr. Pumblechook's, and was immensely relieved to find him not at home. So, leaving word with the shopman on what day I was wanted at Miss Havisham's again, I set off on the four-mile walk to our forge; pondering, as I went along, on all I had seen, and deeply revolving that I was a common laboring-boy; that my hands were coarse; that my boots were thick; that I had fallen into a despicable habit of calling knaves Jacks; that I was much more ignorant than I had considered myself last night, and generally that I was in a low-lived bad way.

I was halfway home, with my spirits thus troubled, before I began to sense a presence behind me. I was possessed with a growing feeling of unease. The woes I had experienced that day made me reluctant to embrace a new source of disturbance but I could not shake off a desire to turn and look. My weariness was forgotten in a sudden surge of anxious energy. I turned my head and for a moment thought that my impression of being followed was nothing but the work of my imagination, still troubled by the encounter at Miss Havisham's. Then, with a growing feeling of horror, I realised that my initial apprehensions were not mistaken. There was indeed a figure following me, a shape I had not seen at first glance because I was looking for a man standing or walking. This was neither standing nor walking, nor, perhaps, was it a man. At a distance of perhaps a hundred yards a shape was slithering towards me along the ground. It was moving with the propulsion of its arms, assisted by convulsions of its torso. It was neither crawling nor walking because it appeared to have no legs. Its face was largely shapeless but its mouth was open and it appeared to be exhaling, or hissing, with all the force in its lungs.

I turned and ran.

This passage made a very disagreeable impression on me. The only possible explanation is that my recollection of *Great Expectations* is inaccurate, and yet that is very unlikely, because my recollection is never inaccurate, and especially not on a question of such particular interest to me as the absence of supernatural nonsense from one of my favourite writer's best books—perhaps I should say, my former favourite writer. I passed an unsettled quarter of an hour turning the issue over in my mind. On reflection, the likeliest explanation, by far, is that somebody at the audiobook company has been playing a joke, a joke in exceptionally poor taste. The prank is particularly bad because it is not inconceivable that someone unfamiliar with Dickens should encounter his work in this form in the first instance, and be left with an entirely misleading perception both of this specific work and more broadly of Dickens's attitudes to para- and supernatural phenomena, and superstition in general. I shall make a complaint.

I have abandoned my attempt to listen to this book, indeed I have gone further and have deleted it. Instead I have, while at the conference and making further use of my superb 4G data

plan, downloaded a copy of *The God Delusion*. I feel in the mood
for an encounter with some bracing plainspoken self-evidently
true atheism. I suppose I can be accused of a form of superstition, in that my wish to avoid reading something superstitious
has led me superstitiously to crave something with no taint of
superstition, however faint! Amusing.

My session is this afternoon. I look forward to the opportunity to correct some idiocies.

## Thursday (continued)

I had not intended to continue my journal today but the afternoon was so strange and so disconcerting I feel an obligation to
record it while events are still fresh in my mind. My session went
as I expected, with the slight exception that although I clearly
carried the day with the force of my arguments, one of the
women arguing for a so called sociological account of economics persisted in repeating versions of what she had said before
I spoke (even though it was plain that I had refuted this line
of 'thought'—I am of course using 'refuted' in the strong and
grammatically correct sense to mean 'proved wrong'). Another
attendee insisted on talking about myth even though I had
shown such an approach to be false. However, the idiotic, like
the poor, are always with us, and it is not that which was the
peculiar thing about the afternoon.

I refer instead to what transpired in the subsequent, final,
session of the day. It was another piece of absurd 'critique' and
accordingly I waited for the first platitudes to wash over me,
then discreetly plugged in my faithful friend, selected Dawkins's
tract and awaited the familiar greeting.

### *The God Delusion,*
### by Richard Dawkins

### Chapter One

However fast I ran, however far I ran, I could not escape the figure pursuing me. Its speed never increased, its mode of loco-motion never altered from its terrible, maimed, partially limb-less slither. I ran and ran, but it never fell behind me, and as night fell, and my strength began to fail, I turned and looked, and saw to my horror that the shape was now closer than it had ever been. It was close enough that instead of a gasp or hiss, I could now tell it was trying to speak, to utter a single word. It repeated the word several times before, with a sensation of ice spreading through my body, I realised what it was trying to say:

'Listen . . . listen . . .'

I ripped the earbuds out of my ears, making a commotion which my immediate neighbours could not ignore. I couldn't believe what I had been hearing. On inspection, the app was clearly displaying my intended selection of book. The corrupted version of Dickens was nowhere to be seen. And yet, that was clearly what was playing in lieu of Dawkins. The only diffi-culty with the forthcoming complaint I will be making to the audiobook manufacturer will be ensuring that it is sufficiently strongly worded.

Well, that's enough excitement for today. I am going to resort to desperate measures and plug the earphones into the confer-ence translation feed for the rest of the afternoon.

## Thursday (continued)

This has now gone beyond a joke, beyond a joke, and is clearly some kind of manufactured attack on my equilibrium. Perhaps it is even a deliberate experiment of the sort popular in the pseudo-sciences such as psychology. I shall be protesting to the organisers in the strongest possible terms. No doubt some form of idiotic 'hack' is behind it. Uncivilised, uncollegiate, unacceptable!

The following is what happened next. At the start of the afternoon session I inserted my earphones into the conference radio apparatus and settled down to listen to some, in the context, soothing nonsense about the equal importance of economics and the humanities. I had skimmed a synopsis of the proposed conversation in the conference programme. The panel was supposed to be debating the absurd thesis that economics merely gives economic models whereas it is the humanities which tell us how we should live, and therefore it is the humanities which should take intellectual precedence. The moderator was Eastern European (in fact was the conference co-chair with the absurd accessories) and the panel members were two Frenchmen and an American. The three Europeans were all talking simultaneously when I plugged in the earphones. There was a moment's pause, which I attributed to the translators' unenviable difficulty in managing the Babel of competing languages, and then I heard:

I reached my lodging with my lungs bursting and my heart racing, unable to draw a full breath or think a clear thought. I do not believe that any man could have outpaced me through

those streets. I tried to take comfort from that thought even as
my mind wrestled with the impossible horror it had seen and
heard. I found that it was difficult even to speak my own name.
I am Pip Gargery, I said, or tried to say, but my mouth was so
dry I could form no intelligent sentence.

And then I heard a noise, a noise I had never heard before
and hope never to hear again. It was a noise of a body moving along the ground, propelling itself with audible effort. The
lower part of the torso was wet and so the thing—I will not call
it a man, though it seemed as though it had once been human—
as it moved, made a slithering, sucking noise. It was a sound
similar to a heavy man wearing waders and walking through
thick mud. I felt an overwhelming sense of cold, not merely
inside my veins, but as if all the air in the room were suddenly
blowing with the coldest of north winds. The slithering, sucking, mucilaginous noise grew closer and louder and then as it
came to the door there was a pause. The silence lasted for a few
seconds. I hoped that the creature's strength had failed. Then
I heard its crying hiss, louder than ever, through the wooden
frame that stood between us.

'. . . listen . . . listen . . .'

The noise, terrible in itself, was followed by an abrupt crash.
The thing had flung itself against the door, which shook and
rattled and seemed set to give way.

'. . . listen . . . listen . . .'


I ripped the earphones out of my ears, my heart-rate danger-
ously elevated and my reason and sense of proportion momen-
tarily flown. The people along from me in my row of seats
looked across; I had clearly made a considerable disturbance.

I did not care. I pulled the earphones out of the device and dropped them on the floor and stood to make my way to the exit. The man on my right tried to stop me to point out that I had left the earbuds behind me, but I pushed past him. My departure made a great deal of noise and under other circumstances I would have gone to great lengths to avoid making such a spectacle, but I had no choice except to get out of that room as soon as I physically could.

Now, writing these words in the complete privacy and partial comfort of my hotel room, it might be expected that I look back on the events of today with recollected embarrassment. Instead I must admit that what I mainly feel, even at this distance, is unease, even fear. I cannot explain this sensation. I am dining alone in my room tonight and will not attend the final sessions of conference in the morning. The taxi leaves for the airport at one p.m. and I intend to be on it and to be writing my next diary entry from my office at the college.

## Friday

Sleep has not come. I lay down and turned out my light and tried to still my mind but the after-effects of my day's encounter with imaginary horrors has been persistent. I can understand having accidentally downloaded a corrupted version of *Great Expectations*, and I can understand how a bug in the app might have over-ridden the subsequent purchase and download of a different audiobook, and I can just about conceive that an ill-meaning hacker, one of the several people at this conference who dislike me and my ideas, might have tapped into the audio stream from the translators' studio, but I cannot conceive how all these things could have happened to me in sequence, even in the most well-resourced and co-ordinated of conspiracies. Brooding on these questions has made it very difficult to sleep.

And now, another persistent after-effect of the day is that in the settling noises of the sleeping hotel, I seem to be hearing things. It is as if, among the noises of people bidding each other good night, trudging up the stairs and down corridors, closing doors and curtains and running taps and flushing toilets, there is another sound, quiet at first but growing louder. It is as if I can hear the movement of a body which is not running or walking or crawling but instead, there is no other word for it, sucking and slithering along the floor. It was a faint noise when I first put out the light but, in the intervals of quiet when the other hotel noises die down, it seems to grow louder. It appears to be coming closer. Now for the first time I can hear other noises besides the muddy traction of a body along the floor, a hiss, or a noise of escaping air, which is, unless I am overinfluenced by what I was hearing earlier today, just possible to make out as a word:

'. . . listen . . . listen . . .'

I have double-locked the door and put the chair against it, with its weight against the handle. Nothing is getting in that way tonight, thank you very much! And yet the slithering is getting louder, and the cry of 'listen' is getting louder too, and all along I can't help feeling that this is bad, this is very very bad, this is rău, rău!, there is nothing I can do to stop this, listen, listen, it is coming it is coming it is

*Notes by*
Dr Frances Scott
Director of Acute Psychiatric In-patient Services
Maudsley Hospital

The preceding document was found on the desk of a 58 year old man, Professor Watkins, who is now a patient in my care. The professor had undergone a psychotic break while attending an academic conference in Romania. He began making a violent disturbance in the middle of the night and was admitted to hospital on an emergency basis, suffering from auditory and visual hallucinations. The hallucinations were acute and persistent. He was sedated and treated with anti-psychotics and five days later was transferred back to London where he is currently under my care as an inpatient at the Maudsley Hospital.

Professor Watkins has been my patient for three months. He responds to sedation but not to other forms of treatment and is docile for much of the time but is still prone to visual and auditory hallucinations. As sudden onset psychotic illnesses go, it is an unusually abrupt and final case but not an unprecedented one. The prognosis is guarded to poor.

One symptom in this case is, to my knowledge, unique. The Professor, however heavily sedated, cannot bear to be in the presence of any kind of paper with writing on it. This psychosis immediately had the most florid manifestations. This symptom is triggered by the merest fragment of script on a post card, is worse with anything printed, and is unbearably acute whenever he catches a glimpse of a book. The staff here have to go to great lengths to avoid this occurrence, because the distress it induces in the patient is both intense and long lasting. It manifests itself in one particular symptom: he puts his fingers in his ears and starts shouting. He always yells the same set phrases escalating in volume until he has to be restrained and forcibly sedated. 'I can't hear you,' he shouts, as if to the book. 'I can't hear you, I can't hear you. You are inaudible.'

# WHICH OF THESE WOULD YOU LIKE?

I can't see a clock so I'm not sure exactly what time the guards come in, but it feels as if they always come at the same time. That would be in character. They're always so polite and friendly and meticulous and they always go through the same sequence. First they tap on the bars to either wake me up or make sure I am awake (I always am) so I can get ready for what's happening next. I sit up and get off the bed and put my hands through the bars and they say, 'Good morning!,' friendly and upbeat, and they put the cuffs on so my hands are stuck on the other side of the bars and I can't move. Then they open the door and come in with the food. It's always the same, not at the other meals but at breakfast: a tray with a bowl of porridge and a piece of toast. No hot drink, I would like a hot drink but that doesn't seem to be an option. At least, when I've asked, the guard just laughs. Then they go out of the cell and uncuff my hands and I rub my wrists, it doesn't hurt particularly and there's no real need but I've got in the habit so I always rub my wrists, and the guards can see me do it, it's become part of the ceremony. I go over to the table where they've put the tray and I pick up the plastic spoon and eat the porridge, and this is the point at which things aren't always the same, because the temperature of the porridge varies, there have been mornings when it is hot, scaldingly hot, too hot to eat, but there have also been mornings when it is cold, which isn't very nice at all, cold porridge is difficult to get down and it seems lumpier than warm porridge even if the texture is really the same, and there are other mornings when it is in the middle, hotter than blood heat or cooler than blood heat but not at the extremes of too-hot or too-cold. I always eat it, though, whatever the temperature. Then, after a stretch of time has passed—just to repeat, there isn't a clock, so I'm not sure, but it feels as if it is the exact same amount of time every day—the guards come back and they go through the same sequence, except this time they don't need to tap on the bars to wake me up because we all know I'm awake. I go over and they put on the cuffs and come in and take the tray and then they uncuff me.

After that they come round with the brochure. Sometimes the guards who do this are the same as the guards who brought breakfast, but sometimes they're different. They bring stools and sit on the other side of the bars. They expect me to bring my own stool over to sit on the other side. Some days I won't do that and just stand there by the bars instead. I can tell they don't like that, but most of the time I bring the stool over. They prefer it when I co-operate, it makes things easier, we all know that. And then they start going through the brochure. Or you could say, we start going through it together. I never know what page they're going to open but there is a sequence and they always move forward in sequence, never backwards, so once I know where they've begun I know what's coming next. They don't always go through the whole brochure, sometimes it's just a page or two, but other times we go right to the end. After the brochure it's always the same, a break until lunch, then they put the cuffs on and I can go for a walk alone in the yard, then I'm left alone in the cell until the evening meal and then an hour or so after that (but I bet it's a precise amount of time) the lights go out.

Today they begin at the beginning, with the mask. I don't like any part of the brochure but the mask is one of the choices I like least. The formula is always the same, they say, 'Which of these would you like?'

'I don't see the reason for a mask,' I say. 'I'm not going to bite and anyway I'm not close enough to bite.'

Usually they just laugh. 'It's always done with a mask,' one of them says today, the younger one. The older man next to him is smiling and nodding too. 'Always! You just have to choose which mask.' And he holds the brochure out again. He is holding it and the younger man is turning the pages. I must say I don't like the brochure, not the content (though obviously I don't like that) but the physical object, a book with coloured pages in poor-quality paper sheathed in plastic, never clean; the paper always looks crumpled and the plastic sheets sticky and sweaty. I do wish it was a nicer brochure. And then the pictures on this page, three on one side and three on another, are all of different kinds of mask, all of them made of metal or plastic (more plastic!) and all with eye holes and nose holes but not mouth holes, except tiny ones about the size of a straw. They have leather straps that go round the back, most of them, but two of them are rubber. They look uncomfortable, there's no chance wearing them could be anything other than uncomfortable, hard to see, hard to breathe. But they insist, they won't go away until I pick a mask, and on different days I pick different ones just to test them, taunt them even, but the truth is they don't mind, they never mind, they just want me to pick one and they're happy when I do.

They move on to the next question, which is what size. They point at small, medium, large, and again they say it, 'Which of these would you like?' Again I change my mind, say different things on different days to mess with them, provoke them, but they aren't provoked, whatever I say, they're fine with it. So I choose a mask and a size, I barely care what, the red plastic one with the leather straps in medium is what I go with today, and they're pleased and they go on to the next thing which is the gown, though here there are only three to choose from and they're basically the same, different lengths but all white gowns with straps down the back and a hole in the middle at the back where your hands stick out. Which of these would you like? I sometimes make this drag out for a while, choosing the gown, to make the point that it isn't really much of a choice, but they don't seem to mind or notice that. They stay good-humoured.

After the gown it's the cuffs. There are six to choose from. One of them is the same as the cuffs the guards use at mealtimes, and they sometimes make a joke about this—'An old favourite here!' or 'Never change a winning game!' or 'The original and still the best!' And there's something in that, I suppose, handcuffs can be very uncomfortable, especially when your hands are behind your back, so maybe it is a good idea to use a pair which you know work without pinching or hurting or cutting off the blood supply. So yes, maybe the old favourite is the one. But here too I spin it out, I try to delay, to look as if I'm thinking about the modern-looking plastic ones with a tie, or the very old-fashioned bronze ones. Today I do what the guards want and go for the ones they suggest, the same ones I use every day three times a day when they come into the cell.

The delays and messing around on my part are for a reason. I'm trying to give the guards the idea that I have leverage, that I can make things difficult for them, that they have an incentive to go along with me, to help me out, that I have some control. That it is in their interest to get along and go along. I'm softening them up, preparing the ground, setting the stage, because what's coming next are the questions I want to ask, the things I need to know. That's why I'm as difficult as I can be at the beginning. I always go through three sets of choices before I ask questions of my own, that's how I do it. I'm not sure why but it just feels right. So today after I've chosen the cuffs and they are happy with my choice—they're pleased with me, I have credit in the bank, I can tell—I ask the question which is always on my mind, the one I'm always trying to get answered. They take back the brochure and start flicking through it to the next set of choices and I say:

'Excuse me, but I have something I want to ask.'

They look up at me, their faces expectant but neutral.

'Why am I here?'

They never even blink. Same expressions. Sometimes they don't answer, not the first time. Other times it's a dialogue. I always prefer that. That's what happens now. Today it's the older one, who's hardly spoken while I was making the choices, who replies.

'Well, that's not really a question for us, now, is it?' he says. The younger one nods, he's in full agreement. Not really a question for them.

'But I don't know why I'm here. If there's a reason why I'm here, I don't remember it, I've never been told. So that's all I want to know, why I'm here.'

The older one smiles at this, he has a nice older-person smile, everything crinkles. That thing where people smile with their eyes, he does that.

'Shall we get on and make some more choices?' he asks. He has turned the brochure to the next page, which isn't an object you choose but a route to the outside, down the corridor to the left and up in a lift or down the corridor to the right and up a set of stairs. Then the two routes converge again so it isn't really much of a choice.

'You make the choices,' the younger man says. 'This is all about you. You're in control. You're in control of everything!'

'Why am I here?' I ask again, arms folded, leaning back. I've dug in, I'm not answering. Not co-operating.

They're both still smiling but there's an edge underneath it now. I like it when that happens, it shows I've got to them, even though they never deviate from their script, if I can sense something beneath the surface it's a sign that something can change, I think, that there are human feelings at work, I've made them show that they feel, even if the only things they feel are small irritations.

'Which of these would you like?' asks the older one, still smiling with the lower part of his face, but his eyes aren't really in it anymore.

'Why am I here?'

This is it, this is the central contest of wills, this is the big
one, the one I'm going to win one day, I can tell I will. This
is the crunch, the crux, the nub, the decider. I double up and
pile on harder.

'Why am I here?'

No pretence of a smile now. Instead he holds my stare, holds
it hard, stares back. He holds up the brochure closer to the glass
and, his voice a little throaty now, says, 'Which of these would
you like?'

I don't speak. Arms crossed, both of us staring. I think about
saying it again but there's no point, he knows what I want to
know. The silence stretches on. It becomes truly uncomfortable.

'Why am I here?'

The atmosphere is changing, in my cell and outside it. I can
feel them getting angrier and angrier. Good. I want that. I want
a reaction. And yet, I also realise there isn't much I can do with
it once I've earned it. They're angry, I'm angry, I'm still in the
cell, I need to know what I need to know and they need me to
get on with my choices. So perhaps this is it, I've done enough,
my point is made. We need to move forward.

'The one on the left,' I say. They don't say anything but they
are relieved, I can tell. Their body language changes immediately. The older one smiles again, his lovely smile. The younger
one nods and his shoulders drop. They turn the page again, it's
clear that they're going all the way through the brochure, front
to back, making every choice. The next page is the one which
really gives you a shock the first time you see it. Hard to take,
difficult to understand. It's fair to say that the first time, the first
few times, you're reeling. You can't take it in. That isn't true for
me now, I'm used to it. But I still remember those first few times.

'Which of these would you like?'

The scaffolds are surprisingly different from each other, given that they all do the same thing, have the same function. Two of them are very theatrical, raised up on mounds, wooden, elemental-looking, one of them especially stark and bare, like a crucifix. Two of them are metal and sit on a low metal platform, almost like a flatbed truck, something you might set up at a market or fair and use to sell your produce. Those ones are much less dramatic, they make the scaffolds look like a piece of agricultural equipment or something. It takes you a moment or two to realise what these are, before you see, oh, yes, that's a scaffold. The last two are flat, made of a material which might be metal (it's shiny) but from the overall aesthetic is probably more likely to be a high-tech plastic. These are scaffolds which look like medical equipment, like a tool designed to get a specific job done.

I hated choosing the scaffold the first few times. The guards knew that, they could tell, it was often a flash-point. Now I've got more used to it and I have a system, I just cycle through the scaffolds in order. I am wrong-footing the whole process, pretending to make a choice but not really. It's a small victory against them. Sometimes it makes me smile to think how angry they would be if they knew. Last time I chose the second one, the taller of the medical-looking scaffolds, so this time I have cycled back to the beginning and I pick the first of the high theatrical-looking ones, where the noose is already set up in place (with the medical ones you can't see the noose). I pick it quickly, and I can tell they're a bit surprised, so I take advantage of the moment to ask a question, my second question, the other one I'm so keen to have answered:

'What did I do?'

At that, the older guard exhales, almost a sigh but not quite, while it's the younger one this time who smiles. The older one holds the brochure, the younger turns the page, and we're on to the hoods for the scaffold, again six to choose from.

'What did I do? Nobody has ever told me what I did. If I did anything, I can't remember, I promise I can't remember. What did I do?'

'Which of these would you like?' says the younger guard.

'What did I do?' I ask again, but I'm not going to have another stand-off, one is enough for a day, I'm just registering that this is a question of importance to me. I think they understand, they don't exactly nod, but nearly, there's a sort of head-movement the younger one makes, down towards the page he's turned, it's as if to say, that is a valid concern but there is also a choice to be made, we need to make some progress here. The page of hoods is to my mind the least important, because why would you care what they look like, you can't see them from the inside, making an impression is going to be the last thing on your mind. Four of them are black, two white, they are different shapes, some triangular and pointed and the others rounder and more sack-like. Here I contradict my process elsewhere, I don't chop-and-change among my choices, I always go for the same one, the round white hood, because it looks biggest and as if it might be the most comfortable, but there's no telling really just from looking at it, you're making a leap in the dark, a pure guess. So we get through this page quickly and then it's on to the final two pages, the guards brisker now, their manner suggesting this is nearly over, as I well know. The penultimate page is six guns, they explain the first few times that this is to put the final bullet in afterwards, 'just to make sure' they say, and I've always thought this part was strange, to give you choices for afterwards when you're no longer here, but that's the way they do it. You choose their tools, it's how they do it. So here I usually go for one of the bigger handguns, because if you did want to make sure you'd really want to make sure and the bigger ones look the likeliest to do that. I choose the biggest today, almost twice the size of the smallest gun, in gleaming chrome, a beautiful object really, that's one of the peculiar things about guns, how beautiful they are, not pretty and not attractive but beautiful. The final page comes next, the oddest of all of them, because this is the only one where you see people, the bodies of people who have gone on before. They are lying in holes in the ground and still wearing the hood and the gown and the cuffs and in some of them you can see holes in the hood, from the handgun shot, but of course you can't tell anything else about them apart from that, you can't identify them. The point is that at this stage the guards take off the cuffs you were given at the beginning and swap them for a new set of cuffs that they put on the body in the grave. They don't explain why. It's a ritual. Apparently they've always done it this way. The cuffs are different, a variety of colours, all plastic, they tie the hands together behind the back and are left like that. As I say, it's a ritual thing. The body in the grave, more of a big hole than a grave, with the new set of cuffs. Black white red, they are the only colours that make sense to me, why would you go for blue green orange for a thing like that?

'Which of these would you like?'

I choose red.

'That's it,' says the older one. The guards pick up the brochure and go away. It always ends briskly. It's like they've paid their bill in a restaurant and are eager to be on their way. I see them walking down the corridor. I'm settling in for the rest of the morning. I know what will happen one day, I hope it won't be today but one day, what will happen is that not long after I've sat on my bed the two of them, the same two, will be coming back towards me, with other guards behind them, and the younger one will be carrying cuffs and a hood and a mask, and the older one is carrying a gown, the very same ones I just picked out that morning, and I will realise that it's today, that the other days were just rehearsal and practise but today is the day. I don't know what I'll be feeling, I expect my body will do all sorts of things at the same time, it'll be physical sensations rather than thoughts or ideas, I expect, it'll be hard to breathe, and then the guards will be at the cell standing there waiting for me to turn my back so they can put the cuffs on. Their faces will be different from before, there will be nothing on them.

I often imagine this. I know how it goes. I don't know how I know this but I do. 'Why am I here?' I'll say, without coming to the cell bars. 'What did I do?' But the older one, his face so hard, I can't put into words how different he seems, he just says, 'No more questions.'

# WE HAPPY FEW

H e waited until the waitress had walked away from the table and was out of earshot.

—I hate that, Michael said. No worries. Why do they say that? No worries. Why would there be any worries? This is a coffee shop. It is literally the entire point and purpose of the place to sell people coffee. So you order a coffee and they bring it to you and you say thanks and they say no worries. Why? Who ever said anything about worries in the first place? It's not like you've gone for an MRI and you're concerned with what the scan shows. It's not like you've been audited and want to know if you're in trouble with the tax man. That's when you want to hear, no worries. When there's a legitimate source of worry, it's fine. When there isn't, it's horrible. No problem is just as bad. I order a coffee, you bring it, because it's your job to bring it, why would there be a problem? Did you just change my flat tyre?

—It's spreading, said Anne. In Paris I've heard them say, sans souci. It used to be the name of the palace where Voltaire stayed when he was visiting Frederick the Great. Now it's a stock reply to some tourist saying merci.

—I believe it was Australian, said Michael. In the first instance. No worries, mate. It's all their fault.

—Literally, said David. I dislike it so much. You just used it. You said, literally the entire point and purpose.

—That has a distinguished lineage, said Anne. It's already there in Joyce's short fiction. 1914. First sentence of 'The Dead.' More or less about a waitress, appropriately enough. Quote, Lily, the caretaker's daughter, was literally rushed off her feet. It has reversed meanings. Now it means metaphorically. Once you realise that you stop minding.

—Well, I haven't, said David. Stopped minding.

Café Jokester was a ten-minute walk from the university's main campus, in the direction of the city centre. It was decorated with large black-and-white photographs of comedians who had died before any of the café's customers were born. This group of friends and colleagues had the habit of meeting there on a midweek afternoon when their schedules gave them a lull that was variously post-lecture, pre-seminar, mid-research. The Jokester had an alcove on the left at the back, a recess that you couldn't see from the main room and which only regulars knew about, and this was their favourite spot. The young academics enjoyed the noise and the bustle of the customers and staff coming and going, the charging up and venting of the coffee machines, the incessant rumble of the traffic outside, and yet they were sitting in their own orderly space, where a trick of acoustics meant they could hear each other without raising their voices. The coffee was good and the cakes weren't bad, but the thing they liked best about the café was this mix of simultaneously being in the midst of people and being on their own.

Jefferson came into the café, stood in the middle of the room and took a quick look around. He caught the waitress's eye and made a squiggling gesture at her which (but only because she already knew what it meant) mimicked the action of somebody applying steamed foam to the top of a cappuccino. He came to join them, sat down lightly and exhaled heavily.

—Seminar go well? said Anne.

Jefferson was teaching an introductory class in general philosophy and it was no secret that he was making heavy going of it.

—Week four. Epistemology, said Jefferson, in his light American voice. So I'm doing the brain in a vat. How do we know we aren't suspended in some fluid, neurons being stimulated to mimic external inputs, identical triggers to those of the external physical world, therefore how do we know reality is real, and so forth. Descartes's demon. Total philosophy 101. And then this student starts up again.

—Descartes's demon, said Michael.

—Omnipotent evil demon who fakes the whole of reality with the intention, the successful intention, of deceiving a single person, said Jefferson. Quote, I shall think that the sky, the air, the earth, colours, shapes, sounds and all external things are merely the delusions of dreams which he has devised to ensnare my judgement. I shall consider myself as not having hands or eyes, or flesh, or blood or senses, but as falsely believing that I have all these things.

—And the victim is the brain in the vat. Got it, said Michael.

—The student was the same one it always is? said Anne.

—Yes. The same one. He starts with, Why a vat?

—Seriously? said David.

—Yes. Why does it have to be a vat? Why can't it be like a really massive jar? Why can't the guy just be plugged directly into something?

—Dear me, said David.

—I know. And then he's like, if I'm a brain in a vat, who are you? And I'm like, well, that's sort of the entire point, that you don't know and have no way of knowing if I'm real or not, and he's like, But that doesn't make any sense because why would you be here if it's just me who exists? I'm saying no that's not the question at issue, it's not who else exists it's whether your sensory input is real, and he's saying, I don't get it. I'm wanting to shout, Yes, I can tell you don't get it—but then luckily one of the others says something and he either does get it or doesn't want to look stupid in front of the rest of them so he stops.

—What did the student say? The one who got him to stop?

The waitress arrived with the cappuccino and put it down in front of Jefferson.

—Thank you very much, he said.

—You're welcome, said the waitress. The three of them who had been complaining about no worries exchanged a glance but didn't say anything. It was their running gag that this waitress liked Jefferson. He took a sip of the cappuccino and sucked a dab of foam off his lip.

—What the other kid says was, Don't think about it as a brain in a vat, think about it as whether the universe is a simulacrum, and you are the only person in the simulacrum. So it's all a construct, made exclusively for you. And he amazingly gets it, just like that. He says, Oh, okay. And we go on from there.

—It's fishy, said Michael. Why would he immediately understand the idea of the simulacrum if he, please forgive the expression, can't get his head around the brain in the vat?

—I know. That's what I thought, said Jefferson.

—I mean, they're the same thing, said Michael.

—They're not at all the same thing, said David, if you think of them as things, a floating disembodied brain in a jar and a colossal all-encompassing artificial computer-created reality—

—No, they're not the same thing but the underlying argument is the same, that's clearly what I meant, said Michael. Clearly.

There was a pause while they sipped their drinks. The city's traffic was building towards the rush hour and the street outside was louder than ever. Horns honked, air brakes hissed, a bus sighed to a halt on its suspension. From the alcove, they didn't have a view of the café's main room, but they could tell from the hum that it was full.

—Is he to be numbered among the stupid? said Michael. That would explain it, if he was just a bit thick. You know, a below-the-line type. An online commentator. Pro-Brexit. Bloody immigrants, coming over here to help our health service. Bloody immigrants, coming here to teach in our universities and win Nobel prizes. Bloody foreigners with their thought experiments about epistemology.

—Maybe, said Jefferson. He has this smirk. When he says things in class, he smirks. It could be a stupid smirk, it could be a knowing smirk. It could be a knowing stupid smirk, he doesn't know how little he knows, maybe it's that thing, that syndrome, the one with the double-barrelled name where stupid people have been proven to overestimate their own intelligence and competence—

—The Dunning-Kruger vortex, said David.

—Yes, that. It could be a Dunning-Kruger smirk. He might be a brain in a simulation in a vat in a Dunning-Kruger vortex.

They all took a moment to think about that, the brain and the simulation and the vat and the vortex. The café was now so busy that even in the alcove it was getting harder to hear; soon it would be too late for coffee and tea and people in search of each other's company would start heading to the pub instead. Over the voices, they could hear the espresso machine venting steam, and the plastic sound of the barista flicking the coffee dispenser to fill the portafilter and then the metallic noises as he clamped it back into place and lowered the pressure lever.

—Maybe he's just fucking with you, said Anne. In other words he's a troll. He's that classic student who's read the next chapter in the textbook and he knows perfectly well about this particular world-famous thought experiment and he's making his own entertainment. Which doesn't mean he's a particularly nice person, but he's not stupid.

—In that case he's studying the right subject, said Michael. All philosophers are trolls. No offence, Jefferson. But that's really the whole project, isn't it? Trolling common sense, trolling reality. What if you aren't real, what if we don't know what we actually know, what if all this stuff we take for granted can't be taken for granted, and what if we ignore all the realities we act on in everyday life and instead push our thinking way past all norms and givens of observed behaviour, into this inhuman domain of pure logic, and see what messed-up and counter-intuitive conclusions we can draw? I mean, that's basically an entire discipline based on a fancy form of intellectual trolling. It's right there at the dawn of the subject. Socrates was the first and worst. Massive, obscene troll. What if the good isn't good, what if justice isn't justice, what if the virtues are really vices, what if nothing is real? Apart from anything else, he's constantly contradicting himself. The dialogues are really just him trolling his mates and them being polite about it. Socrates, the original and greatest troll. He would have loved the comments section.

—Well, people were polite about it and then they weren't and the state had him executed, said Jefferson. Sounds like you kind of agree with them.

—I wouldn't go that far. I just think that if you'd been there at the time he would have been really annoying.

—Socrates looked a bit like a troll, said Anne. Busts of him do, anyway.

—But at least he was arguing with people he knew and not getting into pointless arguments with total strangers in a hundred and forty characters or fewer, said David. Two hundred and eighty characters now but that's really no better, in fact it's worse.

—I don't know if he's on Twitter, said Jefferson. I haven't looked. Not Socrates. I bet he's on Twitter as a parody account. I mean my student.

—You should take a look, said Michael. It's unprofessional not to cyberstalk your students. Everybody does it. Otherwise how do you know what they're saying about you behind your back? Prof Jefferson is a total hottie, heart emoji heart emoji fire emoji kisses emoji.

—He's not wrong, said Anne. They say all kinds of things about us on social media.

—Please tell me you don't cyberstalk your students, said Jefferson to David.

—Of course not, said David. He paused for a moment to

wave at the waitress, who had peered around the corner of their alcove. Could I? he said, lifting his cup. Cappuccino? Anyone else?

Anne nodded, Michael and Jefferson both shook their heads.

—No worries, said the waitress, and walked away. Michael and Anne briefly put their faces in their hands. David shook his head at Jefferson.

—At least, David went on, I wouldn't say, cyberstalk. Nothing like that. But I have on one or two occasions taken a brief look at the online personae of some of my students.

Michael snorted.

—So that's a yes, he said.

—Not at all. Pedagogy implies an interest in and knowledge of the individual student. Engagement on a personal level. This is merely another tool to that end.

—I'm amazed you can bear to, said Anne. It's all so grim. Everything out there is so grim.

There was a pause while they all thought about how grim everything was. It was hard to disagree. Even among people who argued and tested arguments and disagreed for a living, it was hard to disagree.

—Everything about commentary and Twitter and below-the-line is worse, said Anne. Everything. It's like that Miele slogan, Immer besser, but the other way around. Always worse. Immer schlimmer.

—Worse, and making things worse too, said Michael. Remember when the National Lottery was launched and you had ads everywhere encouraging people to take part, or—to use their preferred euphemism—to play? I love that, as if betting on a lottery is a form of play. Anyway. There was a widely made observation that the lottery was a tax on stupidity and then somebody pointed out that way of looking at it was wrong, that taxes tend to discourage people from doing things, so you tax something if you want less of it. But in this case the lottery was treating stupidity as if it was an important national resource, something to be lovingly nurtured and cultivated and given government support. The National Lottery, actively making people more stupid since nineteen whatever it was.

—1994, said David.

—Whatever, said Michael. The point is it's a force for making everything worse by making everyone more stupid. And the same goes for below-the-line, and Twitter and all that. Just people talking complete bollocks all day every day. No, actually, that's too mild—it's not talking bollocks, it's much more toxic. It's lies and abuse and conscious deceit and ill will and anonymous trolling and hate and division and every kind of poison. An entire planet engaged in what amounts to a stupidity contest. That surge in stupidity is the driving force behind everything getting worse, which, let's face it, is what we all agree is happening. And it's facilitated by a whole set of new technologies designed to magnify the worst in human behaviour, the very lowest impulses of which we're capable. Without Twitter there would be no Trump, have you ever thought about that? No Trump, if it weren't for this geyser of lies and boasting and inanities and a systematic assault on the idea that the truth is true and the real is real and decency is decent, all of that made possible by this new medium, one that might have been specially designed to give lies an advantage over truth.

The waitress came back with the two cappuccinos and put them down in front of David and Anne.

—Here you go, she said.

—No worries, said Anne. Michael snorted again. The waitress looked a little taken aback. She collected the empty cups and left the alcove.

—Yes, said Anne. Trump and Brexit and climate change, all of them made possible by lies and stupidity. Orbán and Syria and the People's Party in Poland, and Putin stirring all of it, the worst of us in ascendancy everywhere. The dark rising. Everywhere you look things being objectively and unarguably worse, and made so by our own actions and choices.

—Jesus, Anne, said Jefferson.

—But it's true. The dark in us rising, the dark outside us rising, and all of it being exacerbated by technologies that might as well have been designed to make it worse.

She blew on her drink, tested the temperature with her upper lip, and took a sip. A car driver immediately outside the café must have been boxed in, because he or she pressed the horn and then held it, and held it some more, and for a while it was impossible to talk inside the Jokester, even here in the alcove. The driver paused for a few blessed seconds and Michael opened his mouth to speak, but then the horn started again. Thirty seconds later whatever was annoying the driver must have come to an end, because the noise stopped.

—Bet that man has things to say below the line, said Michael.

—I bet he does, said Anne. She had another sip of her drink and put the cup back in its saucer.

—Designed, said David. I was interested by your use of that word, Anne.

—Explain, said Jefferson.

—Anne used the expression, designed to make it worse, said David. I'm just wondering what she is imagining when she says that.

She shrugged.

—I suppose what I'm saying is if you imagined some force or agency in the world that was leading us towards doom and destruction, towards the dark, and then you imagined what kind of tools and technologies it would use, you'd come up with something like social media. I didn't mean anything more than that. I didn't mean there actually is a design at work. A single mind behind it all.

Two people younger than the four of them, instantly recognisable as students, peered around the corner of the alcove, said, Sorry!, and went away. They giggled to hide their embarrassment.

—Not even people who believe in a God believe in a God who works like that, said Jefferson.

—I never said they do, said Anne.

Michael lent forward and tapped the table with a fingernail, a glimpse for the others of his seminar persona.

—I don't want to leave it there, he said. David is right. Designed. It's suggestive. Think for a moment about what that would mean, if it all were a piece of design. The process of everything having got worse. If we see that process as being intended and deliberate. What would the implications be? You have to head straight for the question, Why? Why designed? And more importantly, by whom?

—An entity resembling Descartes's demon, said David. The word designed implies that.

—Which leads you towards the idea of some kind of experiment, maybe, said Jefferson. The demon is testing something, trying something, fooling around with a hypothesis.

—Unless it's trolling on a cosmic scale, said Anne. An entire universe constructed out of spite and ill will, and, as I was saying earlier about your student troll, making its own entertainment. We are the brain in the vat and the demon is the higher order of reality, and it is fucking with us, just for fun.

—But we know we aren't a brain in a vat, don't we, said Michael. I mean, I know philosophers have been having fun with that idea since forever, and good luck to them, but nobody outside a psychiatric ward has ever truly thought that they are a brain suspended in a vat and all their sensory data is created for them. People entertain themselves with the idea of the universe as a simulacrum, but nobody truly believes it. We all know that we are real, the four of us around this table, don't we?

—Of course, but I'm not sure about the rest of them, said Jefferson, gesturing at the café, at the city, at the world.

The others smiled at that.

—Mind you, Jefferson went on, that is part of the point of the original thought experiment. It might be that those of us sitting and talking here are indeed real. This is easier to imagine if we go with the paradigm of the simulacrum cosmos rather than the single brain. We are four consciousnesses inside a simulated realty, the rest of which is not real, or not real in the same sense that we are.

—Maybe it's the stupid people who aren't real, said Anne. The three men laughed. Seriously, though, maybe intelligent people are the subjects of the experiment and the others are just part of the experimental apparatus. The idea would be that stupid people are simulacrums—sorry, David, simulacra—basically computer programmes, let loose in this simulated reality and given this new thing called social media and encouraged to make everything worse, and then the settings are dialled up a bit, and they get stupider and stupider and the world gets worse and worse and worse, unbearably so, and it's all climate change and Trump and Brexit and et cetera, and the idea, or the entertainment, is to find out how far it goes, how much we can take, to see what the smart people do when they're like rats in a maze but the maze has no way out, is getting narrower and darker and more and more remorseless. Michael mentioned a stupidity contest. People trying to be more and more stupid. But it could be the other way around. Maybe all the stupidity is the test and we're being evaluated on how we cope with it.

—So there could be something a bit like the rapture, said Michael. I've always thought the rapture was a rather amazing idea and that there was no particular reason why it should be limited to the elite of one subset of Christian believers. It's more interesting if it's all the left-handed people who suddenly vanish, or all the gingers, or all the virgins, or all the chess players, anything like that, surprising and arbitrary. Much more fun. So it's like that. The demon changes the settings, tweaks the experiment, and all the stupid people suddenly disappear and the rest of us are left. It would be great! I think. Wouldn't it be great?

—One wonders what the criteria for the rapture would be, said David. I can come up with a few. Anyone who had ever posted a comment below the line. Anyone who has gone on the internet to contest a generally agreed fact or statistic.

—Anyone who has ever posted anything anonymously, said Anne. Anyone who has retweeted something without reading it. Anyone who has ever argued with a stranger. Anyone who has ever sent abuse of any form to anyone, ever.

—Anyone who voted for Trump. Everyone who voted for Brexit, said Jefferson. Anyone who watches reality TV.

—So they get raptured, they vanish from among us, and then what? said David. Let's imagine it's happened, just like that. All the stupid people have vanished. I raise my cappuccino to their memory, he went on, matching his actions to his words and then putting the cup back down. The experiment or the joke or the trolling goes to its next phase as the intelligent people are left behind. I suppose part of the interest would be just how many of us there are left.

—Ha ha, yes, said Michael, I don't think we should get our hopes up.

—And then we'd just have to wait and see what was in store for us, said Anne. Wait for the next part of the experiment, perhaps. Presumably it would have a next part. Wait and see how we cope in a world where there is only us and those like us. What's the Scottish toast? Here's tae us. Wha's like us? Damn few, and they're a'deid.

They smiled and nodded at that but nobody said anything in return. The silence stretched for a moment, and then another moment. They sank into it. The four of them realised that the silence was not just theirs but wider and more general. The café's hum and bustle and clatter had subsided. The brief pulses of noise as the doors opened and closed with the movement of customers to and from the street outside—that had stopped. The traffic seemed to have gone quiet. A short distance away, a car alarm was sounding, on and on, unchecked, an electric sound cutting through the absence of human noise. The space around them felt empty, in the way that an unoccupied house feels empty, with a stillness which is not lack of movement but fundamental absence. This new sensation, this absence, didn't bring a feeling of expansiveness but instead a sudden claustrophobia. All of them realised that they were finding it hard to breathe. They looked at each other, their eyes wild. The clever people could tell that they were all thinking the same thing.

—Rapture is a misleading word, said David. I don't think that's what it would feel like if you were left behind.

—It's fine, said Jefferson, standing up, it's all fine. I'm just going to . . .

He didn't finish his sentence. Michael got up to go with him. He tried to speak but couldn't get any words out of his mouth. He cleared his throat and made another attempt, but failed again. On this third try he managed to speak, but his tone was strange and stranded, and it was impossible to tell if he was making a statement or a question when he said,

—No worries.

# REALITY

When Iona woke up in the house she knew where she was straight away, and she knew she was alone. There was none of that blurry intermediate state of semi-consciousness that people usually get when they're in an unfamiliar place. Everything about the bed, the clean low modern furniture, the white-painted walls, the angled light coming in through the edges of the blackout blinds—it was all crisp and distinct. She stretched and yawned and put her feet on the bare but warm floor. She was wearing her second-best sleeping shorts and some long-forgotten ex's heavily faded Ramones T-shirt. It was a low bed, the kind that older people find it hard to straighten up from. But Iona was not old. Her mouth tasted fresh. She couldn't smell her own breath, nobody can, but she could tell that if she were able to, it would smell sweet. The bathroom was en suite. She padded across to it and surveyed the unbranded but obviously fancy modern toiletries. Fine. She did what she had to do to be ready for the day. She checked herself out in the mirror. Good:

as often when she'd just woken up, she had perfect bedhead. It was known to be one of her best looks.

The next question was: How to fill the day? What next? The others would be arriving before too long, maybe later the same day, maybe over the subsequent days, who knew? But soon. So this was her chance to have a good look around and explore the villa and mark her territory. Not literally, obviously. But a chance to get a feel for the place and to make a good impression. She was very aware of being watched the whole time—that was the entire point of this place, that you were watched the whole time, you are not just on show, you are the show—and that this was a chance to occupy all the space. For today, and maybe for today only, she was the sole and only and exclusive star. It was all about her. Well, okay, then. She would be the star. Eyes to me!

The fitted cupboard was full of her clothes, except they seemed a bit cleaner, a bit newer. It was clever how they'd managed to arrange that. She opened it and studied it and performed complex calculations about how to play this, about what the audience would want and how to give it to them while acting as if she weren't thinking about them and their reactions. Act natural—always a tricky one. First thing, freshly out of bed and on her own: the call was probably for sexy casual, but not too casual and the sexy part mustn't seem calculating. Also, the clock was ticking, she realised as she stood in front of the short wall of clothes. If she spent twenty minutes here and then came out looking like she'd just thrown some stuff on, the extended deliberation would contradict the intended effect. She wasn't stupid. Okay, so it was Lululemon yoga bottoms, the same T-shirt she already had on, and flip-flops.

She hit the switch controlling the blinds. They slid silently up and light flooded into her bedroom. She would look amazing, dazzling, filmed from behind, she knew: a blazing angel. Looking out, she found that she was on the first floor. Outside was a well-kept Mediterranean garden with gravel paths weaving between flower beds, with a hedge about a hundred metres away, and nothing visible beyond. They must be in a high place, not overlooked. There would be a pool, Iona felt sure. It was a compound. She could see no way in or out. So perhaps this was the back of the house.

Iona headed out into the stairwell for a bit of an explore. This upper floor of the villa had six rooms leading to a gallery, with stairs running down one side and a skylight above and walls painted white. It was very bright. She knew without looking that the other rooms would be bedrooms, and that this meant there would be six of them in the villa. Three girls and three boys. She couldn't see any cameras or mikes, so whatever they did with them must be very very clever, super-clever. Her consciousness was—had to be—double at all times: what she was doing, and what impression she would make by doing it. That was fine by Iona: she was used to it, she knew how it worked. She knew the rules of seeming. In accordance with them, she went and tapped briefly on the door of the room next to hers, waited a few seconds, and nudged the door open. As she'd expected, everything about the room was identical to hers. She didn't bother checking the other rooms, not yet. There was no shortage of time.

Downstairs Iona found a hallway that opened out under the gallery and gave direct access to a huge sitting room stuffed with beanbags, a TV room, what must be intended as a boys' room with game consoles and a pool table, a lovely big kitchen with a breakfast bar and dining table. Another large room opened straight out to the—she'd been right—huge bright blue-green swimming pool, where there were six sun-loungers laid out under umbrellas on one side, six laid out in the sun on the other side, and a pool house at the far end. It looked like, indeed was, a picture-perfect holiday pool. She went out, dipped a hand in the warm water, walked around, felt the colossal fluffy towels in the poolroom.

All this time Iona was thinking hard. People might be interested in what she did with herself when she was by herself but they wouldn't be interested for long, so it wouldn't be more than a day at most. She must think of it as one day at a time. She must look composed, sexy, self-contained; mustn't look needy and impatient for the others to arrive; must look like someone who can look after herself. While taking care at all times to act natural. What that meant in the short term was that she should make some breakfast. She hadn't checked that the kitchen was stocked, but it must be—it would make no sense for it not to be.

She flip-flopped round the edge of the pool, crossed the room that led from the pool, pushed the kitchen door open, and almost died of a heart attack. A dark-haired woman was bending down and looking into the fridge. Iona's scream made the woman startle and she hopped up and shrieked too, making a dissonant off-beat one-two of female distress. The woman put her hand on her chest and took a breath.

'Jesus! I'm sorry,' Iona said. 'You startled me. I thought I was on my own. I'm Iona.'

'Nousche,' said the woman, who had the trace of an accent—French? Italian? That must be her name: Nousche. She was wearing a light, filmy top and clinging shorts. These looked

carefully calculated in a sexy Eurominx style, while also being
fully deniable, as something she had just flung on in the morning without a second thought. Nousche's dark hair curled round
her face, a very sophisticated bob cut. Iona couldn't tell why but
she had been sure the next person in the villa would be a man.
That was just how shows like this worked—girl-boy, girl-boy.
Evidently that was wrong. If it was going to be a girl, though,
this kind of girl was perfect: dark where Iona was blonde, petite
where Iona was tall, classy-foreign where Iona was relatable-
native. Maybe it would be all girls, calibrated to be different,
like a manufactured pop group. 'I saw you down by the pool,'
Nousche went on. 'I was just coming out to say hello but I
wanted to see if there was anything to eat first. I'm starving.'

'Me too!' Iona said, though it wasn't strictly true: she'd been
too hyped and energised by the strangeness of it all to think
about food. But it would make the wrong impression if she
seemed like the kind of girl who was too up herself, too interested in being skinny, to admit she needed to eat. The calculations she was making about first impressions were all changed
by the arrival of the second girl. She wasn't creating an image of
how she behaved when she was on her own, but giving a sense
of what she was like to interact with. Very different. Now it
was time for Operation Nice. Well, that was no problem. Iona
knew how to do nice.

'What is there?' she said, bouncing over towards the cooking
area. She noticed that the acoustics of the kitchen, indeed of
the whole villa, were hard and flat—no soft surfaces, nothing
to absorb noise.

'Everything,' Nousche said, opening the fridge wider. Something about the way she flung the door open—or pretended to

fling the door open, because you can't really fling a fridge door open, not without breaking it—made Iona see that she had a feel for drama; Nousche was one to watch. Good to know. Iona, playing along, peered into the fridge. It was indeed very well stocked, which was a good sign because it meant the others were coming and were probably coming pretty soon.

'I could make us a frittata?' Nousche said. Damn, thought Iona. So Euroskank gets to be the practical caring helpful one, while also avoiding carbs.

'Super!' said Iona. 'You know what, while you do that, I'll just check the other rooms, because if you're here and I didn't realise, maybe some other people are here too, you know, and we can ask them down?' This would serve the dual purpose of making her look caring and thoughtful too, while also getting her out of Nousche's blast area for a bit so she could formulate a plan.

'Unless they need a lie-in?' said Nousche, counter-thoughtfulling. Oh, okay, bitch, so this is going to be war. It was always easy for an observer to pick up on overt bitchiness, snark, eye-rolling, and you didn't need to counter it, because the cameras and mikes countered it for you. But this was much more subtle. Nobody would have seen anything yet. They wouldn't know what was happening.

'Well, I'm sure your frittatas are delicious,' said Iona, 'it would be a pity if anyone missed them!'

Nousche did a weird thing closing her eyes and raising one shoulder. It seemed to mean something along the lines of: Oh, all right, then, if you insist on flattering me so, please by all means go ahead. Iona went back to the main staircase and started heading up. Part of her wanted to change clothes, to signal to herself that the game was different; but that made no sense. In fact it would just look a bit mad: girl meets other girl in villa, changes outfit. No, Lululemon had got her into this, and Lululemon would have to get her out. She climbed to the top of the stairs and went past the door she had already checked to the one after it—and just as she was reaching for the handle, it opened from the inside and a man stepped out. Iona didn't give a full scream as she had when startled by Nousche, but she did emit a squeak. The man had curly red hair, lots of it, and was of medium height and compactly built, a fact it was simple for Iona to verify because he was naked from the waist up. A gym bunny, it was easy to see. He was carrying a towel in his left hand, and now flung it across his shoulder to cover himself partly, an impromptu toga.

'Whoa,' he said. Semi-posh accent, a bit like Iona's own. 'I thought I was alone. Harry.' He held out his hand.

'Iona,' said Iona. 'I thought the same thing. But you're the third. And maybe there are more, I haven't checked. Nousche is downstairs, making omelettes. No, frittatas.' This was, Iona thought, so much better. While Harry wasn't her type—nothing personal, she could see he was attractive, just not for her—there was no denying that this was much more like it. Balance and order had been restored to the cosmos. It would surely be half boys and half girls now, anything else would make no sense. On this terrain, she was sure she could prevail.

'What's a frittata?' said Harry.

'It's an omelette that's gone wrong on purpose.'

'Cool,' said Harry. 'I mean, I'm allergic to eggs, but still, you know, cool.'

In that moment, Iona felt that she loved him very much.

Harry gestured back towards his room. 'I'll just, you know, clothes,' he said.

'Absolutely!' Iona said.

———➤———

So they had breakfast together. Iona ate enough of Nousche's frittata to show she was a good sport, but left just enough to show that it wasn't particularly good. Nousche did an I'm-French, I-eat-everything-and-never-put-on-an-ounce thing. Iona (caring, practical Iona) made Harry a bacon sandwich. They chatted about this and that, but mainly about when the others would arrive and who they would be and what they would be like. It went unstated that they would be attractive young people, because, well, it was obvious that that was the whole point. They talked a bit about what they did before. Harry was a model. Nousche was a 'gallerist,' whatever that was. Iona thought about asking her, but her instinct was that the query might not come out right—might sound like an attack, which was problematic, because of course that's exactly what it was. So she would save that for later when the lie of the land was clearer. Iona told them she was an actress, because if she said she was an actress slash model slash influencer ('classic triple threat,' according to her agent) that would make two models out of three and would thereby hand Nousche an advantage.

Just as they were finishing breakfast, Eli walked into the room. Iona had screamed when she saw Nousche and squeaked when she saw Harry, but honestly, when she saw Eli, she almost fainted. He was so far past handsome it was like they needed some whole other vocabulary for it. He had long black hair which was at risk of being cut by his cheekbones, dark brown eyes, and was wearing a white linen shirt which did an exceptionally bad job of hiding just how ripped he was. Best of all, he carried himself as if he weren't aware of any of this—just, you know, moving through his day, Nothing to see here; it's normal for girls to cross their legs and become unable to speak, I'm sure that was what it was like before I came in. Iona wasn't sure how they got through the introductions and all that: she could hear the blood in her head. Crucially, she could tell he preferred her to Nousche. Nothing specific, she could just tell. Ha!

Eli was a photographer. Not a fashion photographer, the other sort. You know, war zones. Of course he was.

After breakfast they went for a swim and to hang out by the pool for a while. Iona was a very good swimmer—a very elegant swimmer—and had been looking forward to this being a point of difference, but it annoyingly turned out that Nousche was a star swimmer too. Still, Iona knew she was on strong ground with the impression she made in a bikini. She did a few laps, then got out and dried off in the sun on a lounger next to Harry. He was lying on his front to tan his back, but when she lay down he turned over and flipped his Ray-Bans down over his eyes.

'Dude, gonna be honest, I could get used to this,' he said.

It was too bright to open her eyes and too warm, in the direct sun, to think or speak clearly, so Iona made an affirmative grunty noise. The problem of how to fill the day, this first day, had been solved by the new arrivals, each coming as a pleasant surprise, unexpected to her and no doubt to the viewers too. Or maybe the viewers already knew? No—no point thinking about that too much. If you were constantly trying to second-guess the audience, to see what they were seeing and finesse or manipulate it, you would go mad. And also you would be obvious about it and that would spoil the whole thing. You can't be seen thinking about how you seem—fatal. Still, it was tempting to wonder if they knew what was coming, who would be next through the pool room, who would be next to do the self-conscious walk, the self-conscious wave, to reach up and flick their long black hair out of their dark brown eyes, to pull off their white linen top and . . .

A tall black man came out from the house and stood in the doorway by the pool squinting over at them with his hand held up to shield his eyes from the sun. He was wearing a grey T-shirt and black sweatpants and he too was super-ripped, even more so than Eli and Harry, which Iona wouldn't have thought was possible, but this guy was something else, it was like his muscles had muscles. Also, he seriously knew how to make an entrance. He did a slow look around and then walked over towards them. Nousche stopped swimming, came to the side of the pool and draped her arms over it, the skank. He went towards her, crouched down on his haunches, held out his hand and said:

'Liam.'

Nousche held out her hand in an unbelievably pretentious way, wrist up, palm drooping down, like she was the fucking queen or something. She said her name. Liam did a squinty smile and—this too was unbelievable and was all Nousche's fault—briefly bowed his head down and kissed her hand. Iona felt she might throw up in her mouth. Liam straightened up, not without a lingering flirty smoulder towards Nousche, and came over to Iona. Get up, don't get up? But if Nousche had done a duchess number, the thing to do was go the other way. Iona hopped up off her lounger and walked towards Liam. Harry, nice manners, got up too. Harry was closer to Liam than she was, so they greeted each other first, Liam offering a fist bump and a 'Hey, man' that couldn't be more precisely judged to be Harry's shtick. This new guy was a very quick reader of people. He came over to Iona and said hello and then came in for a quick unsexy people-person's hug.

'Well, this is weird,' Liam said. They all agreed it was weird. 'Is everybody here?'

'I don't think so,' said Iona. 'Six bedrooms. Five of us so far. Three boys. So I'm guessing another girl? But I don't know any more than you do.'

'I doubt that's often true,' said Liam, giving her a private smile. Iona knew enough about players to know how it works: you flatter the clever ones for being pretty and the pretty ones for being clever. And yet she still felt a complimented glow. Would it be so bad if it stayed at five in the villa, three boys and two girls? Would that be so very wrong?

'I wonder when it'll start,' said Harry. 'You know, tasks, whatever it is.' He flexed his shoulders, thinking about tasks.

'Me too,' Iona said. 'What did you do, what do you do, out there?' she asked Liam, trying to guess: Athlete? Not another actor; he was the wrong kind of vain.

'Money,' said Liam, with a smile. 'I do money stuff.' That meant banking or finance or something, and don't bother your pretty little etc. Nousche had kept swimming, but she must have realised she was being left out of the chat, so she got out of the pool, wrapped a towel around her head and came over.

'We're just talking about when it will all start,' said Iona, being the friendly one, because she could sense, in the patterns developing, that that would work for her. 'You know—'

But Nousche knew what she meant. She was nodding vigorously.

'Tout à fait,' she said. 'I was wondering—' and then she was interrupted by a loud female voice coming from the pool patio.

'Wahey!' it said. 'Room for a small one?' A tall strong-looking girl in a black tracksuit and baseball cap came bouncing—no other word for it—out of the villa and crossed to the pool. Iona instantly thought: Here comes the noisy one. The new arrival strode over to where they were standing and said:

'Oi oi! I'm Lara but everyone calls me Laz.' They intro- duced themselves in turn and, in turn, Lara/Laz came in for a full hug and double-cheek kiss, including with the still pretty damp Nousche, whose expression was that of a person having second thoughts.

'Cor, you're soaking!' said Laz. 'Mind you, I am too now. I should tell you, I'm mainly straight, but I'd be lying if I said I don't sometimes like a bit of both!'

All the men suddenly looked interested. Nousche looked as if she might be about to burst into tears. Iona said: 'Shall we go inside and have a cup of tea?'

They spent the afternoon continuing to wonder when the tasks would start, what they would be like, when the evictions would begin. The format is always that some time will pass before the first evictions, at least a week, maybe more. It might be two weeks or could even be as long as a month. Of course they would be watched and listened to, monitored and judged and assessed, all the time. It was the nature of these things that some of the tasks would be humiliating, physically or psycholog- ically. Break the six down a bit, get a sense of what they're really like. Or—to put it as an opportunity rather than a problem—

give them a chance to show a bit of grace under pressure. Just as
a hint about the nature of the process, the huge library of DVDs,
which looked so promising at first glance, consisted exclusively
of box sets from reality TV shows. It was the British Library of
reality TV. Talk about a strong hint for what was to come.

The thing was, though, that the tasks never started. The housemates talked and talked and thought out loud and ran alternative
scenarios about what might be going to happen to them, but
none of it did. They were all wondering when it was going to
start. Perhaps the problem was that they were too self-aware, too
aware of the setup; perhaps the problem was precisely that they
were talking about it so much? It could be that there was a taboo
on asking these question out loud; it was making them seem too
needy, too conscious of the audience. In short, maybe they were
doing something wrong. It was vital to think about the viewers
all the time. It was also vital not to seem to be thinking about
them. To Iona this was an interesting conundrum for the first
day or two, but gradually more oppressive. She was having to
work hard at it and could tell that the others were too. She had
a theory, one she hadn't shared with the others yet: that this was
a new kind of show, one where there was no interaction with
the producers or the viewers, no games or tasks or challenges
or external organisation, no structure. They wouldn't be told
what to do. They would just be evicted, expelled, one at a time.
It could start at any point. They were waiting for it to start, but
perhaps it had already started. Just a theory, but it could be true,
and if it was true, Iona had figured it out, but was pretty sure
the others hadn't.

The pool was okay, because you could just lie there, or dive in when it got too hot. Her room was okay, a sanctuary, the only place in the villa where she felt she could just be herself, by herself. Though that of course wasn't entirely true; they were being watched, and the moments when you were on your own could reveal a lot about who you were. You had to be particularly careful about the amount of time you spent primping and floofing. You didn't want to underdo it so badly you looked like you'd been dragged through a hedge, but on the other hand you didn't want to be caught seeming vain, taking too much trouble, pouting and striking poses. But nobody changed their minds about someone because that person was sitting alone in their room. You need to get out there. So Iona did get out there.

It was the kitchen and dining room that were difficult. The issue she had noticed on the very first morning, about the acoustics, was more and more prominent. It was the flat hard reflective surfaces that caused the trouble.

Iona's father had been a poker player in his youth (a very good one, according to him), and he had once said that the best way of telling whether someone was telling the truth was to listen not to what they were saying, or even to the tone of their voice, but to the echo of their voice. In this sharply echoing indoor space, the coolest room in the baking-hot villa, Iona began more and more to notice the sound not of the other contestants' voices, but their echoes. The voices would often be lifted, bright, happy, joking. The echoes sounded flat and angular and full of silences; full of holes, contradictions, meanings that weren't supposed to be there. Positive greetings—'Hi!,' 'How are you!,' 'Love the outfit!,' 'Looking good!'—sounded like curses or lies. The echo of a joke sounded like an insult. The echo of a friendly question sounded like a jeer. The echo of a friendly comment dripped with loathing. They spent lots of time in that kitchen. And yet when you spent time there you came to think that everything about the villa was the opposite of what it seemed to be: that good feelings were full of hate, that friends were enemies, that laughter was violence, that there was no such thing as love.

➤

On the morning of the seventh day, Iona woke early, a shaft of light from the corner of the blind catching her eye as she rolled over in bed. The spectacular Balearic light was one of the principal characters in the villa. In the morning it was slanted, yellow, insistent: Get up! Show yourself! Act natural! It wasn't the kind of light that made it easy to lie in bed. Nobody came out on top in a contest like this by lying in bed. The morning sun here reminded you of that. Then, as the morning wore on, the light gradually hardened. From midday through the early part of the afternoon the light was so bright it was almost metallic. It gave you thoughts of escape, because you knew there could be no escape. The sun was like a giant staring eye. There was no colour to it, just pure light. However much sun cream you put on, you could feel yourself cook. Getting out of the pool into the sun you felt like a lobster climbing into its own pan, fizzing and sizzling.

The way you could tell this part of the day was coming to an end was by seeing colour start to return. The white sky went blue, the blazing vertical light started to tilt and turn silver, then yellow, then, as the day turned to evening, gold. The colours of the garden and villa and the contestants and their clothes looked like themselves, only more so. Everything was lovely in that brief period of glow, especially the six of them, during that golden hour which here was shorter than an hour; but they were never more aware of being filmed, surveilled, watched and judged and assessed and ranked for popularity.

Allegiances and alliances were covertly forming. Iona couldn't say anything explicitly, of course, but she knew that she could do a lot with body language and eye talk, with grunts and nods and even silences: silence of assent, silence of letting something hang there, amused silence, disgruntled silence, disbelieving silence, drawing-someone-out silence, silent disagreement and silent disobedience. Iona always got on best with intelligent people. That meant the person she should be getting on best with in the villa was Liam, who was clearly and self-evidently bright, and—it made her grit her teeth to think this—Nousche. But that didn't work. Liam was a game theorist, that was Iona's take on him: an angle-player, a manipulator and reader of rooms, and to make it worse the person he got on best with—was always having tiny muttered colloquies with, side-of-the-mouth—was Nousche. As for Nousche, well, she was still and always Nousche, still her incredibly annoying, permanently calculating, dissembling, sneaky, undermining Eurosnake self. So the people with whom Iona would normally have clicked most easily were not only not her friends, but were in an unnerving alliance with each other. As for the others, Harry in a sense didn't count. He was good-natured and weak and not very bright. They got on well but Harry was like a dog: he would get on well with anyone who petted and fed him (which incidentally was something they had to do, since Harry was the only person in the villa who never cooked anything; you wouldn't trust him to be able to make toast). She was left with Eli, who was so good-looking it was distracting, and was one of those men who have never had to learn how to talk, because women are always fainting and falling into bed with them on sight. So he was off-the-scale attractive but also exhausting since you had to do literally ALL the conversational work. This meant that the person she got on best with was Laz. That would be a surprise at first sight, but it was much less so once you'd seen Laz at close quarters for a day or two. She was noisy and up-for-it to compensate for a secret self that was private and shy.

When Iona got downstairs to breakfast on that seventh day, Laz was already in the kitchen, stirring something on the stove.

'Oi oi,' she said, but quietly.

'Oi oi,' said Iona, also quietly. 'What are you making?'

'Porridge. "Keeps me regular," ' she said in a voice which made it obvious she was quoting somebody, even though there was no possibility that Iona would know who it was. That was one of Lara/Laz's habits and it meant that at times, for all her outgoingness and good nature, you couldn't tell what she was saying, beneath the various layers of impersonations, special voices, ironies and mini-playlets. 'No carbs for me,' she now said in a different voice, one which could, just possibly, be an impersonation of Nousche, in which case Iona officially thought it was hilarious.

'Moi non plus,' Iona said, joining in the anti-Nousche moment, but not too obviously, just enough that only clued-up viewers, and Laz herself, would know what she meant, if that indeed had been what she meant.

'Are we the first up?'

'Herself and Liam are doing laps,' Laz said, making vague waving gestures with her arms, possibly indicating breaststroke.

By using 'herself' to mean Nousche, it was clear that she was drawing lines. This was an escalation. Oh, it's on! Iona sat down at the breakfast counter. She was having a little think. The best move was probably to egg Laz on while not appearing to, while also sending signals that she was on the same side, but not coming across as too much of a mean girl. Bitchy but deniable.

'Laps before breakfast,' Iona said, her tone making it both a question and a statement. 'Laps after breakfast. You know—bit of curd. A few berries.' Iona didn't roll her eyes but she flared them slightly, in on the joke but subtly so.

'Fancy some porridge?'

'Why not?' Iona said. Laz put the saucepan she'd been stirring on the breakfast bar, then followed it up with bowls and spoons and sat opposite. She dolloped porridge into the bowls, pushed one across to Iona and started blowing on the bowl in front of her.

'I vant some berries,' Iona said in a German accent, for no other reason than that she thought Laz would find it funny, which she did, very.

'Get your own focking berries,' said Laz, also in a German accent. They snorted and giggled together and the noise (and entertainment) they were generating was enough to distract them from the arrival of Harry, who had come downstairs and into the kitchen barefoot and topless. In a villa full of good-looking, not-shy people, Harry stood out for his uncanny, almost supernatural body confidence.

'Guys,' he said, as a greeting.

Iona held up the saucepan, offering the porridge Laz had made.

'Um—yeah, cool,' said Harry. He got himself a bowl and

spoon and helped himself. His arrival threw the dynamics out a little, since he could be absolutely relied on to miss all the nuances about trash-talking and ganging up on Nousche while pretending not to. He didn't speak while eating his porridge but gave little nods of appreciation.

'Man, that was great,' Harry said when he finished. 'You could like, open a restaurant.'

'A porridge restaurant,' Iona said, giving Laz a look. But Harry, while slow, was maybe not as slow as all that, because he immediately said: 'Is that funny?'

'No no,' said Iona, flustered, cornered, stalling. 'No, it's only—'

'Because lots of restaurants do nice breakfasts. Brunches. People love it.' Harry said this sulkily. The encounter was turning into a disaster. Iona and Laz were being turned into the mean girls, which was completely unfair—well, okay, it was a tiny bit fair, but they weren't specifically being mean to Harry at this point, they'd just got a bit carried away over their bonding.

'People love breakfast!' Iona said, maintaining eye contact with Harry while, as it were, directing her mind at Laz, who was supposed to pick up on this new tone. 'I just thought it was funny to have a restaurant that only did porridge, you know, like for the Three Bears or something. You could call it the Three Bears.' Again, there was that thing with the echo. Her voice sounded normal when you listened to it, but if you paid attention to the echo, you would think you were hearing a soul in torment, pleading, angrily begging, for release. A terrible noise. Harry, though, had a ginger's trained awareness for when he was being picked on. He didn't say anything, just took his bowl over to the sink, washed it, put it on the drying rack. Iona and Laz looked at each other and Laz gave a tiny eye-shrug. This exchange wasn't reparable, not immediately.

Iona was thinking hard about how this would look, about what her next move or gesture should be, but before she could come up with anything, Liam, dripping slightly, came in from the pool in his swimming trunks. He was rubbing his hair with a towel. He had the air of a man who knows perfectly well that this sight is to be considered among the eight wonders of the world.

'Sup,' Liam said, not really making it a question, still towelling away.

'The usual,' said Harry, his tone neutral on the surface, but the echo hissed. Liam gave Harry a look that showed he knew perfectly well what Harry was talking about. He nodded. Iona realised with horror that 'the usual' meant her and Laz ganging up, being the baddies, the bitches, the self-appointed alphas. This could only mean that Harry was already aligned with Liam and Nousche! They had thought they were being careful: they hadn't been anywhere near careful enough. Oh, this was a disaster! If that was how it seemed to the housemates in the villa, for the viewers it would be a hundred times worse. Everything would be magnified, blown up, replayed, commented on. It was literally impossible for this to have gone more badly wrong.

And then it did, because Nousche came in from the pool. Having done the look-at-how-little-I-care-about-being-seen-with-wet-hair thing on the first day, she was now a genius at always having her hair completely on point. Of course, that style, the Louise Brooks thing, was easy to manage, but . . . Iona could feel herself getting distracted and forced herself to snap out of it. This was a crisis. She could die on a raft with

Laz or she could maybe, just maybe, cut herself loose and float to safety. Groups often have an official scapegoat and outsider. New name for that person: Laz.

'I wish I hadn't had that porridge,' Iona said, puffing out her cheeks, making a fat-person face. 'Bloat city.' Nousche didn't stoop to answering that observation, not with actual words, but she did make a tiny little moue, a sub-pout, of agreed amusement. Iona thought: This could work. Don't overplay it. Subtle. That's how you crush it, in a situation like this—with subtlety.

'Yeah, you sure don't want to live there. Bloat city,' said Laz, doing one of her silly voices, her cheeks puffed out the same way Iona's had been, and Nousche laughed, and then the others laughed too, including Eli, who had come downstairs during all the breakfast drama without Iona realising he was there. Iona started to join in the laughter, though in truth she didn't fully get it, and then she realised that Laz's silly voice was actually an impersonation of Iona, and she saw, with a feeling that the floor was sliding down from beneath her, actually physically sinking down and down and down, descending into the earth—she saw that all of them were laughing at *her*. Laughter, that was what it was supposed to be. And yet, if you listened to it in the new way, by paying attention to the echo, it didn't sound like laughter at all. It sounded like the noise made by souls in torment; by beings undergoing torture; it sounded like screams of pain and anger, like nails on a blackboard but in physical form; it sounded demonic. There was nowhere to go outside this noise. The laughter grew louder. Iona moved towards Nousche and then past her and stood in the doorway to the pool and turned to face them. All the housemates were standing in front of her. Nousche was closest and the others were behind her. The light was already taking on its harsh, burning, middle-of-the-day flatness. The laughter had taken on its own momentum; they were still laughing, were laughing harder than ever. What did this mean, where did they go from here? What would the viewers think? How would this look? How would they be judging her? And still they kept laughing at Iona, all of them lined up, as the laughter and the sound of torture grew and grew, the sound of souls screaming in pain grew louder and louder, as they stood there, all of them—Iona, Nousche, Harry, Eli, Liam, Laz—and then with that feeling of dropping through the floor, free-falling, nauseous, the roller-coaster plunge in her stomach, the noise of torture in her ears, she got it: Iona, Nousche, Harry, Eli, Liam, Laz. I—N—H—E—L—L.

They could all see her distress, indeed they seemed to be actively enjoying it, but of all people it was Liam who broke things up. He came over to her and put a non-sexual arm on her shoulder. Nousche came further into the room. Harry moved out towards the pool. Laz was doing something at the sink, Eli had turned and gone back upstairs. The dynamic changed and, as with a shaken kaleidoscope, the old pattern had been permanently erased. Iona must have been imagining things, imagining the feeling in the room, and everything else too.

'Hey,' Liam said, his voice low, 'you okay?'

Iona didn't think she was, but she nodded. And in truth she did feel a bit better. The others were talking, not loudly and not consequentially, just chat, and it was helpful to listen not to the echo but just to the words, not the undertone but the tone.

'It'll begin soon, okay?' Liam said. 'The tasks and evictions, they'll begin soon. It's not as if this will go on for ever.'

She listened hard to his voice, just the words on his lips. The difference between forever and for ever: she'd been taught that at school. Forever, as in someone is forever going on about something. For ever as in endless, lasting for all time, continuing for eternity. For ever. She listened to what Liam was saying and felt herself believing it; they'll begin soon, it's not as if this can go on for ever. Nothing goes on for ever. Does it?

# COLD CALL

've always disliked it when people say that some person or object or place is the best or worst example of something 'in the world.' It makes me want to object: How do you know? How can you possibly know? That pistachio ice cream from the gelato shop on the Piazza Navona might be very nice but have you eaten every other flavour of ice cream from every other ice-cream shop, counter and van on the planet? No? Well then perhaps it's better not to say it is 'the best ice cream in the world,' merely that it is very very good ice cream. The best you've ever eaten—that's fine. Just not the best in the world. I'm not saying it couldn't be the best in the world, just that you couldn't know it.

This is the reason why I'm not going to claim that my husband's father is the most annoying person in the world. I have not met everybody in the world. I can't even claim that he is the most annoying person in Europe, or the United Kingdom, or England or London, because I haven't met everybody in all those places. What I can say is that he is the most annoying person I have ever met, or heard about, or read about, or seen depicted or alluded to in any artistic medium. I have never encountered a fact or anecdote or any form of evidence that a more annoying person exists or has ever existed or ever will exist. But that is not the same as saying he is the most annoying person in the world. Though, just to be clear, I'm pretty sure he is. But I'm not going to make the claim. That's an important distinction. I'm a lawyer. I get paid for making distinctions like that.

What I'm talking about here isn't the normal irritation of being in the sandwich generation. This is generally defined as being in the intermediate age group who talk to their children and their parents using the same tone of voice. Now, there's some truth to this description, insofar as it involves tone—though that's where the similarity ends, for me at least. In all other respects, talking to my children, who are ten-year-old non-identical twin boys, is very different from talking to my father-in-law, who is eighty. The big difference is that I don't hate my children. In the course of talking to my sons, I don't start quite badly wanting to kill them. In the last decade, I have never had an interaction with my father-in-law which did not involve me wanting to murder him.

Apparently men are often told that they should meet a woman's mother before marrying her, because that is how she is likely to turn out. If women were told that, and I had met Gerald, I probably wouldn't have married Tom.

Example. Five past eight on Monday morning. As any working parent with school-age children knows, that is a highly charged moment in the day. That week was particularly difficult. I was in the middle of defending a complicated fraud case and had been up studying the brief from five o'clock. My husband is a film producer and was on location in South Africa. (My best friend from university once took a long slow drag on a pink Balkan Sobranie, made a long slow exhale, and gave me the following life advice: 'All mothers are single mothers.') I had thirty minutes to complete the children's toilette, dressing, breakfast, school-gear checklist, and get out of the house in order to be at my neighbour's house in time for the car-pool lift to school and then head to the Tube station to be at chambers on time. There would be parts of the day that were more intellectually demanding than this, but none that would involve more stress. At this exact moment, the phone rang.

We don't have caller ID. We don't need it. Everybody calls me on my mobile. The only people who use the landline are cold callers and my father-in-law. I prefer the cold callers, because I can tell them to piss off and immediately hang up. I picked up the phone in my right hand: I had my day's briefs in my left hand and was holding a packet of cereal pinned to my right side with my elbow.

'Hello?' I said, thinking: Please try to sell me something. Please, go on, I beg you.

'Yes,' said my father-in-law. Although he calls often—sweet Jesus, does he call often—he never acts as if he has initiated the call. His demeanour when he rings is that of an exceptionally busy person who has been interrupted in the middle of a demanding and important task that there's no point explaining because anyone stupid enough to interrupt him is by definition too stupid to understand.

'You called,' I said—and then there was a microscopic pause during which I faced the fact that I've never fully reconciled myself to calling my father-in-law by his first name, while at the same time looking on with fascinated horror at the family lives of friends who call their parents-in-law 'Dad' and 'Mum'; my preferred term for him is 'you'; but sometimes you have to take the plunge—'Gerald?'

'The letter about parking,' he said.

I executed a quick memory check. My father-in-law's issues with parking make up a thick mental file, a very thick file, an entire cognitive filing cabinet. It was one of his most frequent topics of conversation. (I had been going to say 'favourite topics of conversation,' but the word 'favourite' would imply that it was a source of pleasure, and Gerald does not express pleasure). While I could remember complaints about how expensive parking is in the borough, back in the day when he could still drive and therefore still had a car, and complaints about the fact that parking in the borough was so cheap that anyone could now do it and everywhere was permanently crowded (after he stopped driving), and complaints that cars were parked very badly, and that the wardens were nothing but thugs in uniform, and complaints about the fact that the police were nothing but traffic wardens with the power of arrest, and complaints about the number of parking restrictions in his street, and the number of spaces taken up by removals and building work—while, in fact, I could remember complaints about more or less any parking-related activity about which it was conceivable to complain, I couldn't remember anything concerning a recent letter about parking. What that meant was most likely that he had discussed the topic with Tom. When Gerald wanted to, he treated Tom and me as entirely interchangeable, so that if one of us knew something, the other was expected to know it too. He was also capable of treating a conversation with either one of us as subject to the same rules of confidentiality and non-disclosure as a state secret. It depended on what, in any given situation, would create more difficulties.

From upstairs I heard a small thump, then a louder one, then a slamming door, and could hear one of the twins crying, not loudly. The quieter the cry, the worse the trouble; louder cries, designed to attract parental intervention, were more tactical.

'Gerald, I'm so sorry, this is an awkward moment, I've got to get the twins ready and off to school, can I call you back later?'

He exhaled, with the air of a man who had been braced for disappointment but was nonetheless disappointed to find his expectations so thoroughly fulfilled.

'I don't know, can you?' he said, and hung up.

No jury of my peers would convict me.

I put the phone down, put my brief in my work bag, put the cereal packet down, ran upstairs, dried tears and adjudicated a fight and made peace and fixed up breakfast and checked school-bags and got everybody out the door in time and began the day.

At various points on that Monday I found myself thinking about Gerald. My client, the defendant in the fraud case, was called Tony. He is a classic 'cheeky chappie'—a line I may well find myself using in front of the jury. He is lively, funny, jokey, flirtatious, easy. That's what made me think about Gerald: because he's the opposite of all that. He doesn't smile. I have never heard him laugh. He does not express happiness, or satisfaction, or relief. He does not praise. I once asked Tom what Gerald had been like as a father, and he replied with a long, cold, un-Tom-like look, before saying, 'What do you imagine he was like?' Tom's mother died when he was a teenager, no doubt from being worn out by her husband; Gerald then got through a second wife, who died ten years ago, since when he has lived alone. Tom's sister moved to New Zealand straight after university, and never comes back.

Ah, yes—university. Gerald read history at Oxford University. As with most people who went to Oxbridge, his policy is to tell you about it within thirty seconds of first meeting, and then remind you about it at ten-minute intervals until one of you dies. I have heard him say many times that in the first-year history examinations, the lowest passing grade is 'vix satis,' abbreviated to 'vix sat,' meaning 'scarcely satisfactory': 'a very useful term,' according to Gerald. The implication is clear. For Gerald, most of life, most experiences, most people, are vix sat. Including his daughter-in-law.

My mind returned from Gerald to my client. One of the ways to get a defendant off a fraud charge is to make the fraud seem extremely complicated and invite the jury to conclude that your client is too thick to have pulled it off. The purpose of this meeting in chambers was to chat to Tony a little, and see whether this line was likely to work. The solicitor knew perfectly well what I was at. He and I had worked together many times before. At the end of the meeting, he and Tony left the room together, spent a few minutes talking outside, and then the solicitor came back in and sat down again. We sat in silence for a moment.

'I'm not sure,' I said.

'Too sparky,' he said.

'It's marginal. He could dial it down a bit in the dock. But it's risky. He's doesn't come across as Forrest Gump.' I didn't like that film much, though from a barrister's point of view its hero would make an ideal defendant in a complex fraud trial.

'A big boy did it and ran away,' said the solicitor, meaning we should perhaps run the other principal line of defence in fraud trials: that the defendant was coerced or encouraged or misled by more senior figures. In cases involving financial institutions, this line has the advantage that it is sometimes true and (more important) that juries are willing to believe it.

'Yes. There's stuff we can use. Maybe we, meaning you and your colleagues, can find a bit more.'

'Okay,' he said, and left.

One of the things you learn if you have young children and are a de facto single mother with a demanding job, is the effective use of time. I have 'help,' obviously, but even with a nanny picking the boys up and making their tea, I still try to get home to see them before bed, and I make a point of having at least one day a week when I greet them at the school gate and take it from there—and often end up exhaustedly working long after their bedtime. This Monday was to be one of those days. That meant I only had until three p.m. in the office, and that in turn meant I was using super-power levels of concentration all day. I do sometimes wonder if I actually get more done on these days, when the clerks know to defend me from every interruption below the level of a burning building, and hardly any of the emails I write are more than three words long. As the deadline for going home comes closer, I accelerate. Then I run run run, out of chambers to the Tube, run to the platform, run from the platform at the other end, jump in the car, fume in traffic to the school, park illegally, grab and hug my boys and take them home, and then be weektime Mummy for a few hours.

After all this, with the boys in bed and my work laptop out on the kitchen table and the single glass of weeknight wine poured, just as I was thinking, So that was Monday, the phone rang. I suddenly remembered that I had forgotten to call Gerald. It was a quarter to ten, though, which is outside what he calls 'courtesy hours.' So this wouldn't be Gerald, meaning it must be a cold caller. I sometimes have fun with them, but it was late and I was tired and not in the mood, so I let it go to voice mail. This normally makes them hang up, but whoever was on the other end of the line held on and starting talking into the answering machine, so I picked up.

'We're registered with the telephone preference service, it's illegal to call unsolicited on this number,' I said in greeting—as I've already explained, it was late and I was tired.

'Is that Mrs Porson?' said the voice on the other end of the phone, using my married name.

'You called me—if you don't state the reason why, I'm going to put the phone down now.'

And that was how I found out that Gerald had had a fall, and been lying on the floor all day, more or less since he had called me in the morning. He had a cleaner's visit scheduled that afternoon. He doesn't trust his cleaner enough to give her his keys, so she came to the door and rang and waited and rang again and then went away. She cleaned someone else's house, but providentially, after doing that, decided that something wasn't right, and went back to Gerald's. After ringing a few times she called through the letter box. Gerald called back and she heard and rang an ambulance, and Gerald was now in Chelsea and Westminster Hospital. I got a neighbour to babysit and spent the rest of the night in the emergency ward. As for the next day at work, well, let's just say there's a reason why God invented Red Bull.

Gerald's fall came with an upside, a downside, and a score draw. The upside was that Tom temporarily came back from his shoot in South Africa. Gerald needed someone around and for work reasons it couldn't be me. (Our marriage needed it too, but that's a different story.) Gerald had home help and had in the past had live-in help too, but he was so difficult that nobody stayed for long and there were long stretches during which he was on his own. He was a few miles away from us and refused to downsize or move closer, so when he asked for help he was asking for the specific task, which took anything from five minutes (change a fuse, change a battery) to thirty (write and post a letter, do something on the council website) to several hours (build furniture, do weekly shopping and prepare food for invited company so he can show off). In addition to this was the transit time, which when there was no traffic, i.e., never, was half an hour each way, and more often was forty-five to sixty minutes each way, so that five-minute trip to put new batteries in the remote took two hours plus.

The downside was that Gerald was now clearly in need of more help. That meant more demands, more visits, more back-and-forth, more trouble. The score-draw was that Gerald needing more help was a good thing, to my mind, because it meant Gerald was nearer to that bright shining day when he would be forced to admit he wasn't fit enough to live on his own and would have to move into a home.

I'm aware this makes me seem like a terrible person. All I can say in response is, you don't know Gerald.

He was in hospital for a week and when he came out was set up with a new gadget, attached to a cord around his neck: an emergency button to trigger an alert to a call centre, who would in turn call us. We had a meeting at his house with a man from the alarm company, who set it all up with our home and mobile numbers. There were two levels of care, one where they automatically send a paramedic on a motorbike, and another where they call you first, you call the client, and then if all is not well they send a bike. We chose the second, lower level. He explained everything and then asked if we had any questions.

'I'm not deaf and I'm not stupid,' said Gerald. After that the man packed up and left without a word. And then our new life began, the one with Gerald a mere touch of a button from making us have to drop whatever we were doing and rush to help him.

Within two weeks, I had learnt to dread it when I looked at my mobile and saw the number of the health-alarm-alert company on caller ID. Tom had gone back to South Africa, claiming that if he didn't he'd be sacked and/or the production would run into the sands. The fact that our marriage was running into the sands didn't seem to count for much. Any marriage is a couple against the world, and the world often wins. Often it wins through sheer force; it just has so many tools and techniques. I was juggling work, the children, and my newly urgent task of sitting in on interviews to find Gerald a live-in helper. In addition, Gerald used the alarm call facility to get hold of me when I was in client conferences (because he was feeling dizzy), when I was in the bath (to find his TV remote), and when I was on the school run (I never did find out what that was about, because I was stuck in traffic and already grouchy, so I hung up on him). The only place he couldn't call and get hold of me was in court, because you can't take your mobile into court, thank God in heaven and all his saints.

The second time the number came up in a client conference, like the first time, I was with my fraudster, sorry, 'alleged fraudster,' and his solicitor. I stepped out of the room to take the call. This meant talking to the alarm company, then calling Gerald.

'Yes?'—Gerald's standard greeting.

'What is it now?'

'I'm unwell. Is that of any concern to you?'

'Gerald, I'm at work, and this thing is only supposed to be used for emergencies and it doesn't sound as if this is an emergency.'

'As I said, I'm unwell.'

'You sound fine.'

'I have a fever.'

'How do you know?

'Hot.'

'I'm in a meeting. I'll call you back.'

I hung up and went back into the conference. All women know the feeling of realising that in their absence something has taken place among a roomful of men. There was an awkward atmosphere and the solicitor cut the interview short after about fifteen minutes. Then he went out for a talk with his client, as per their usual practise, before coming back in for a bit more time with me.

'Diana,' he said, in a special leading-up-to-it-carefully voice.

'Skip it, Alan,' I said.

'He wants a new brief. Sorry.'

This happens, everyone knows it does, but it doesn't happen to me often.

'Fine. He give a reason?'

'You're asking?' Meaning, did I really want to know. I nodded. 'He says you seem distracted. Sorry.'

I thought, Well, fuck you very much. I also thought, Thanks a lot, Gerald. I said:

'That's showbiz. See you round, Alan.'

'Diana,' he said. And with that he left, and my multi-week, multi-thousand-pound fraud case left with him. I sat back in my chair and gave in to some dark thoughts about how little I was enjoying my life at that particular moment.

I don't often call Tom at work, not once he's on location, because there usually isn't much point. When he's on set his phone is turned off, and when it's turned on, it's because he's using it. Producing a TV programme is an all-day, every-day process of problem solving and firefighting, even when the programme you're making is a pile of shit. This mid-budget, by-the-numbers fantasy series wasn't the worst thing Tom had ever worked on, but it was by his account pretty bad, and he was doing it purely for the money. In my more forgiving moments I could feel a little bit sorry for my husband, and see that the high-stress constant hassle of filmmaking in the service of a knowingly mediocre product is hard on the soul and the psyche.

On the off-chance, I rang him, hoping he'd be available but not expecting it. To my happy surprise, he picked up the phone on the third ring.

'Hello, darling, I'm having a shit day,' I said.

'What did you notice?' said Tom, street noises behind his voice.

'I don't know what you mean, and whatever you do mean, I'm not in the mood for twenty questions,' I said.

'Please—what did you notice when you rang?'

'You answered. For a change.'

'Anything else?'

'Oh, please, darling, I already said I was having a horrible day, your father is ringing me every fifteen seconds and the kids are being a nightmare and I'm not sleeping and I've just been sacked by a client for the first time since Labour were in power, so I know you love twenty fucking questions but your timing is off, okay?'

Give him credit, he did not wither on the vine.

'Notice anything about the answer tone?'

'I'm hanging up now.'

'It rang twice. South African ringtones ring once. That was a UK ringtone. The reason being, I'm in the UK. In fact, more specifically, I'm in the Pret across the road from your office. I was going to burst in and surprise you.'

'Tom!' I said. I don't often look, think, feel or behave like a teenager in love, but I threw the phone into my bag and ran out of my office and downstairs from chambers and across the street, and flung myself into the arms of my husband.

➤

'It isn't an emergency,' said Tom at lunch, sitting catty-corner across from me in the restaurant where we went on our first significant evening out, where he proposed, and where we've been for the three anniversaries when he wasn't on location and

I wasn't exhausted from children/work. He picked up the crab claw he'd been eating, fiddled with it for a little bit, realised he'd already finished it, and put it back down. 'It's just a difficult patch.'

Subject: our marriage. I had thought we were just scratching at familiar sore spots, but Tom clearly thought it was worse than I did. Well, he would know. A relationship is as good as the least keen partner thinks it is.

'And that's why you came home,' I said. I was on glass of wine one-point-five and could feel myself on the verge of becoming either romantic or belligerent. This could go either way . . . The hum and bustle of a busy lunchtime service is a thing I've always loved, even when my mind is elsewhere, as it was now. Our waiter came and cleared our starters while I waited for Tom's answer.

'We had a crisis on set. The lead's partner found him having sex with a makeup girl. Caught them in the trailer, like something out of a sitcom. They had a huge fight, threw things at each other, now our star has a four-inch gash across his face and can't shoot in close-up for two weeks. I took the opportunity and here I am.'

'I thought he was gay.'

'So did I. So did his boyfriend.'

Tom can always make me laugh. The main courses arrived and as I looked down at the filleted sole, gleaming in a slick of herbed butter, I felt something inside me go soft and forgiving. The principal difficulty in my life was Gerald, and it wasn't fair to blame Tom for his father—if anything, it was a reason to feel sorry for him, having had that man at the centre of his existence for four decades. I could see Tom sense the change in my mood. He took off his jacket and hung it over the back of his chair. He smiled.

'I did a bad thing.'

In the private language of our marriage, this means the opposite: it means he has done something spendy and parent-centric.

'Okay.'

'I've booked us a hotel room and fixed the nanny to stay over.'

The feeling which swept over me, I was surprised to find, wasn't pleasure, or horniness, or excited anticipation of a new treat, but relief. I suppose that without realising it, I too had started to think that our marriage might be in real trouble. Tom knew it, I knew it. But the fact that we knew it was surely a sign that we could grab the handbrake before the vehicle rolled over the cliff. A relationship can deteriorate past the point of no return without anyone having realised. If you know it's happening, you have a much better chance.

'What about the kids?' I said, not so much because I was genuinely worried, more that it was part of the maternal job description. 'It'll freak them out if we're just suddenly not there.'

'We'll call them after school. Say you came to meet me at the airport and we stayed the night there. Something like that. They'll be pleased I'm home, that'll cover it.'

Tom got up, came round the table, and kissed me, soft but firm, unmistakably a kiss with sexual intent. It felt very good indeed. He straightened up and headed for the loo. I sat back in my chair. If I had been a cat I would have been purring. A switchback of a day so far: normal, then very bad, then very good. If you're eating fish in Sheekey's with the person you love and are halfway through a bottle of Chablis and are about to spend the rest of the afternoon having sex in a hotel, even if you're the kind of person who isn't much good at counting her blessings (I like to joke that I don't have time)—still, good moment to get out the happiness abacus and tot 'em up. And just as I was thinking that, my phone rang.

I got it out of my handbag: the alarm company. Gerald. No leisurely lunch, no catch-up with Tom, no skyrockets in flight oooooh afternoon delight—instead, Gerald. With that thought, I found that I had declined the call. Then I switched off the phone.

A buzzing came from across the table. Tom's phone was vibrating in his jacket pocket. I reached across and killed the call, then turned off the phone and put it back in his pocket. They would call at home too, in fact probably had already, but there wasn't anybody there and wouldn't be until after school, so we still had a couple of hours.

Tom came back from the loo. He was wearing my favourite smile, sexy and a little sly.

'Happy, darling?' he asked. I had a mouthful of wine so instead of talking I gave a thumbs-up.

➤

They say that sex in a stable relationship follows the rule of six, two, two. Six times out of ten it's really nice, two times it's nothing special, and two it's great. This was one of the latter two times. We lay snuggled up for a bit and then Tom went for a shower. I yawned and stretched in bed. Mixed sensations were competing for my attention: a post-orgasmic glow versus a post-lunchtime Chablis crustiness. In an ideal world I would have a snooze and when I woke might still have the glow, but the crust would have worn off and I'd be ready for the evening. But it was quarter to four and the boys would soon be home from school, so I needed to get on with it.

My bag, knickers and bra were all on a chair in the far corner of the room. It was impossible not to check myself out in the full-length mirror en route. One of life's underrated pleasures, to look good completely naked in a full-length hotel mirror.

'I'm just going to check in that everything's on course for pick-up,' I called out to Tom, and turned the phone on. Imagine my surprise when I saw there was a missed call and voice mail from the alarm company!

'Shit, darling, I missed a call from the alarm company,' I said. 'They rang while we were fucking.'

A good detail makes for a good lie.

'He probably can't find his slippers,' yelled Tom, from the shower. 'Once they missed you because you were in court, so they called me in Cape Town. I called him back and he was ringing to complain because his books-for-the-blind tapes were a day late.'

I got my worried voice ready and rang the alarm company.

'Hello, I'm so sorry, I'm a registered contact for Gerald Porson but I missed a call from you a few hours ago.'

I waited on hold for a bit while he found the records.

'Excuse me for a moment,' he said. Muzak, for a good couple of minutes. Then a different voice, an older woman, came on the phone.

'Hello, is that Mrs Porson?' she said. I braced myself for a bollocking about missing the call, and maybe also for a bollocking about Gerald having abused the service, but I was braced for the wrong thing, because what she told me was that Gerald had had a small stroke and fallen, followed by a bigger stroke, after which he had died.

➤

The next few days were hard. I'm not making it about me (at least I don't think I am) when I say it was more difficult for me than for Tom. He had mourned the loss of his father—the absence where his father should have been—many years ago. That gap, that lack, was part of who he was. So he was fine. Sad because something had never been there, rather than sad for the loss.

It was different for me. I had spent years struggling with my feelings about Gerald, emotions which ran on the spectrum from irritation and dislike to outright hate. I had sincerely wished him dead many times. Now that my wish had been granted, I felt not that I had wronged him in general, but that I hadn't done the thing Tom had done many years ago, and let myself feel sad. Something had gone very badly wrong with Gerald's emotional wiring, either through his upbringing (about which he had never spoken, not once, and about which Tom knew nothing) or just the luck of the genetic draw. But the fact was that this man who I deeply hated was a sad man who had lived a sad life, and had died alone.

That last was the hard part. On the Piccadilly line, Gerald is, I mean was, less than fifteen minutes away from the fish restaurant where Tom and I were having lunch that day. We could easily, very easily, have been there in his last moments. The paramedic on the motorbike was delayed by another call—a drop-everything chest-pain emergency—and took an hour and twenty minutes to get to the house. On a normal Gerald call, there would have been no consequences for that, because on a normal Gerald call all he needed was for someone to tell him where to find his good pair of slippers. But this wasn't a normal Gerald call. There was another thought, one that I found, what's the word, not so much difficult or painful as aversive: one that I occasionally let myself glimpse by opening my eyelids an infinitesimal fraction, before clamping them closed again. That was the possibility that if we had gone straight there as soon as I'd got the alarm call, and had seen that Gerald had had a stroke, we could have saved his life. I don't know that for sure, and I certainly didn't want to put myself in the position of knowing, in case the knowledge turned out to be something I didn't want to live with—but I just caught the edge of that possibility, at the hospital when we went to see Gerald's body, and in the follow-up call with the alarm company. It wasn't anything they said or didn't say, it was a space or silence around their words. I'm a lawyer, I can tell when people are being careful but letting you catch a hint if you want to. Maybe, if I'd done what I was supposed to do, Gerald would have made it.

The effect of this was to make me feel guilty. I didn't want Gerald brought back to life, and if I could press a button and have him back on the end of the phone calling me whenever he felt like it, I wouldn't. I want to be clear about that, so I'm not being hypocritical. But I did feel guilty. It's not an emotion I'm familiar with, guilt. It doesn't feature in my life. The law has clean-cut rules and clean-cut outcomes, and that's what I like about it. I love the fact that you obey the codes and do your best for your clients and at the end of the process you either win or lose. I don't carry feelings from my work around with me. That's for the clients—after all, they're the ones who're out there doing things. But I felt guilty now. I felt that I had done wrong, that I should have done different, that I had consequences hanging around my neck. I felt, God help me, like a defendant.

This was made worse, much worse, by the fact that I couldn't tell any of it to Tom. I realised, too late, that the moment when I could have done that was straight away. If, as soon as we knew that Gerald was dead, I had burst into tears and told my husband I had done a bad thing and felt wretched and how could he ever forgive me, I think there is a good chance he would have told me he'd have done the same thing himself. He was randy and half-cut and furious with his father just as I was, and he too would have killed the call and gone to the hotel room for a fuck and woken up to find he'd accidentally killed someone. He would have forgiven me there and then. But none of that happened, and as each day passed it became more and more unthinkable to turn back and try to undo the secret I was keeping.

The funeral and cremation were at Mortlake. I'd been there a few times before, but never for a relative. There was nobody there apart from us. Gerald's will, which he had left in immaculate order, had no instructions for the service, so we kept it short and simple. We chose a Bach partita for the accompaniment. Gerald didn't like anything written much after Bach: he disliked music that, in his words, 'reeks of the human.' The boys, with their dark suits and ties and pale faces, looked as incongruous as Bart Simpson with his hair slicked down. Gerald's coffin went through into the crematorium fires. I knew we'd be getting the urn two days later. We came out into the early dark and as I took Tom's arm to squeeze I felt my phone, which I'd forgotten to switch off, vibrating in my bag. Tom felt it too and gave me a look.

'Sorry, darling, just let me take care of it,' I said. I took the phone out and, as I killed the call, was hit with an irony: the caller display was from the alarm company. They must be calling for a—inappropriate word in the context but I knew what I meant—post-mortem. We stood on the porch for a few moments, the children in that uncomfortable mental space where they knew they were supposed to feel appropriately solemn emotions, but in truth just wanted to get home to resume their never-ending fraternal struggle on *Smash Bros*. It was cold outside the crematorium. Gerald wouldn't have minded that. He liked the cold.

'Home,' said Tom. We stopped for a transgressive McDonald's drive-through on the way, and ate it in the car in our funeral best. When we got home the boys took off their ties and went straight on to their console. Tom went upstairs to do some admin. He was going back to South Africa later in the week. I fired up Spotify, tried to find a playlist I liked, couldn't, poured a glass of Manzanilla, decided I didn't want to drink it, got out a couple of cookbooks to try and think of something to make for dinner the next day, realised I was still too full of Filet-o-Fish to think about food. Gerald's short, bleak service at the end of his long, bleak life had left me unable to settle.

The phone rang. I couldn't be bothered to answer. I re-changed my mind about the sherry and swigged it down in one. I went through and gave the children their fifteen-minute warning before bedtime. I was wondering if I would go through the rest of my life with every missed call reminding me of that other call, the one I had declined on purpose.

I found it hard to sleep that night. That sometimes happens when things are quiet; stress makes me aware that I need sleep and good habits, whereas when I'm less busy, as I was now thanks to having been sacked (thanks in turn to Gerald), my sleep hygiene is worse and my unconscious asserts itself more. I toss and turn, I fret and fidget, I drift in and out. I checked the time on my phone—always a mistake. The night was excruciatingly slow, as such nights are. In accordance with one of insomnia's cruellest tricks, I slid off to sleep around dawn.

An hour or so later I jolted awake. I was certain that the phone call had been from Gerald. It couldn't have been from Gerald, of course not. And yet I was certain that it was. I can't say how I knew this, but I did. My chest was tight with shock. I wanted to wake Tom to tell him what was happening, but as I reached out to him, I realised that I couldn't—that my feelings would be too easy to dismiss, unless I revealed to him why I was so troubled by the thought of Gerald reaching out to me. He had done it while he was dying and he was now doing it in death.

I didn't sleep any more that night. The same thought kept running through my mind: Gerald was trying to ring me. I held off the terror by telling myself that this couldn't be true, and as dawn turned to day, that felt easier to believe. The insomniac's curse: a wave of fatigue and need to sleep broke over me just as it was time to get up. I was so shattered and ratty that the twins took fright and were uncharacteristically prompt and obedient.

Tom was at home and there wasn't anything I knew about waiting for me in chambers, but I couldn't face spending the day in our house, flinching at the telephone, so I went in to work. Before setting out for the Tube I turned off my mobile and put it in a kitchen drawer. Try getting hold of me on that, Gerald.

I told the clerks not to put any calls through and spent the day doing a mixture of half-necessary admin and busywork. I left early to avoid the rush hour and found that Tom had shopped and was cooking one of the four things he could competently make, roast chicken. That was fine. While he was getting something from the store cupboard, I went to the landline socket and unplugged it. We had supper. I hovered nearby while the boys did their homework. We jointly dried them after their baths and jointly got soaked. The plan was to watch some grown-up television together, something we hardly ever got the time to do, since there weren't many evenings when I didn't have a brief to read. It didn't work because I was just too tired. I apologised to Tom and staggered upstairs at half past nine.

A few hours later I woke with the same jolt as the night before. I got out of bed, put on a dressing gown and slippers, and went downstairs. My phone was still in the drawer and the master socket was still unplugged but I couldn't shake the feeling that I had to hide from Gerald's call. I needed brightness and noise. In the kitchen I switched on all the lights, put on the kettle, turned on the radio. I needed voices, not music, so I twiddled the dial until I found what is normally my least favourite form of listening, a radio phone-in. Raised voices were trying to yell over each other in a shouted non-conversation about immigration or Trump or whatever. It was, for my purposes, perfect.

Quarter past four. Even for a person not prone to imaginary fears, the small hours are the worst time of the day for phantom terrors. There was no chance I'd be getting back to sleep, so I made myself a strong builder's tea. The kitchen is the room in our house where I spend more waking time than anywhere else, and it's also my favourite room, so being there helped me start to calm down. Routine would soon reassert itself and everything would be fine.

The phone began to ring.

At university, I had a tutor who told me he wouldn't walk through the college library at night—he was a Fellow, and Fellows had their own keys—not because he was frightened of encountering anything supernatural, but because he was 'frightened of seeing something that wasn't possible.' I had laughed, but had also known what he meant. I knew it even better now, in this moment.

Our house has a basement which we use as a children's playroom. This was once full of stuffed toys and beanbags; now it's a haven of electronics and video games. I slammed the kitchen door behind me and ran down the stairs, my tea sloshing out of the mug. I pressed myself into the far corner, the cold walls against my back and shoulders. In the corner of the room, in the depths of the house, I was secure and safe. Nothing could find me here, nothing could get me here.

Just to my left there was a small pile of discarded, un-used and under-used plastic toys. Plastic cars, soldiers, guns, dinosaurs, space rockets. I had made several attempts to throw all of this detritus out over the last couple of years but the twins were passionately opposed. They didn't want to play with this old stuff, but they wouldn't let me chuck it away. I'd even, twice, filled a black binliner full of unloved toys, en route to the recycling plant, and twice been intercepted before I could get to the car.

As I pressed myself into the corner next to this pile of plastic, I heard a sound I hadn't heard in years: the jangling ring of a toy phone. This was a wind-up toy given to the boys by Tom many Christmases before, with an unmistakable trilling ring. It couldn't be that, because the phone hadn't been wound up in years. And yet there it was. I knew immediately what it meant.

I reached out to the toys and pushed the top ones—a truck, a tank, an aircraft carrier—to the side. A small landslide ensued and now the toys were spread all over the floor. The phone fell to the floor with a crack. It was still ringing—not like a real phone but with a thin, plasticky, grating vibration. It was bright green and had two buttons, a yellow one marked Answer and a red one marked Hang Up. I picked up the phone and held it to my ear. It kept ringing. I counted to ten, and still it rang. I thought to throw it against the wall, smash it to fragments, but then I thought this would keep happening, this would never stop, and there was only one thing I could do, so I pressed the yellow button: Answer.

'Yes?' said the voice on the other end of the line. I didn't say anything.

There was a pause, which stretched into a silence of perhaps thirty seconds. Then there was a sound I knew immediately, an unmistakable sound, even though I had never heard it before. A sound I had thought did not, could not, ever exist. It was a wheezing, gasping, exhaling noise, starting quiet and growing louder; this terrible thing I had never wanted to hear, that no other living person had ever heard or ever would hear, the wholly unfamiliar, wholly horrible, instantly recognisable sound of Gerald's laughter.

# THE KIT

Jarlath came downstairs in the morning and found that the device had stopped working. The kitchen was full of morning light, gleaming with the new day, an extra glitter from the dew outside making it seem as if the room were flickering with life. That made all the more contrast with the broken old equipment standing immobile in the corner between the sink and the fridge. It had failed suddenly, as they do, though now that Jarlath had hindsight he could see there had been little glitches and flutters and signs that this moment might be coming. Still, there had been no warning the night before, and there was no point pretending it wasn't a surprise, and an unwelcome one. Jarlath sighed and went to put on the hot water and hoped that this wasn't going to be one of those days, full of unexpected small things that went wrong.

He took some bread out of the bread bin, cut a slice, turned on the grill and waited for it to warm up. All actions that he would not normally have to do for himself. Jarlath reflected that in principle, once he'd got used to the idea, he was not unhappy at what had happened. He liked change and liked challenges, and this was not the first time he had been through this process—was, if he thought about it, more like the sixth or seventh. He thought back over the previous models, the small improvements and upgrades over the years, and the small dis-improvements which came with them. There was little point in feeling emotion about old gear, but the fact was that he did. He felt the same about old cars, about his first tractor—but he didn't feel like that about his second tractor, because it was still in use. Now, that was a good tool, battered and patinated with time, but working as well as it ever had . . .

The dance was always the same dance. When the old kit wore out, Jarlath's instinct was to wait for a while before ordering a replacement. It was something he liked to do with any piece of equipment, even with furniture: take your time and work out what you really need. If your sofa breaks, and you immediately order a new one, the chances are you'll get one that's pretty much the same—same form, same function—as the one you've just got rid of. That, for Jarlath, was a missed opportunity. This is your chance to ask, what is a sofa for? How do we use it? How would we live differently if we didn't have one, or if we had a different one, or if we used the living room in other ways? If you just steamed straight ahead and replaced worn-out stuff with new stuff, you skipped your chance to ask those questions. So if it was up to Jarlath, he would wait, make do without for a while, do things for themselves, take the learnings that came with that. They might want the new model to do different things from the old model, but how would they learn what they wanted if they didn't give it a bit of time?

Of course, Jarlath knew well that it wasn't entirely up to him. His paternal authority depended on the fact that he didn't rely on that authority all the time. He rationed his use of 'because I say so.' But his four boys tended to feel differently when it came to anything affecting their convenience. When the device wore out they always wanted to get a new one straight away. An uncharitable person would say that was because its absence involved them in extra work, and they were young people, to whom extra work was always de facto a bad thing, to be avoided. Work, Adam's curse, Adam's fault, Adam's gift to his descendants . . . Jarlath was old enough to disagree with that. What would life be, what would a typical day be, without work? Not a holiday, because a holiday depended on its difference from the days around it. But the boys were still young and didn't see it like that.

While he was thinking about the boys, the youngest of them came down the stairs, Jed taking them two at a time, as he had been warned at least a thousand times not to do. Jed had only just finished school and begun work on the farm—full-time work, as opposed to the jobs he and the others had been doing in their spare moments since they were old enough to walk. He came into the kitchen and looked at his father standing at the cooker spreading butter on his toast; then he looked across at the broken-down unit and blinked with realisation.

'Oh, man,' he said. Jarlath cut another slice of bread and put it under the grill for his son. 'I'm going into town tonight. I was going to have a snack before. Now who's going to make it?' said Jed.

'Looks like you are,' said his father. Jed pouted, his expression that of the child he still was but deeply wanted not to be.

The sight made Jarlath sure that he was right and that the family needed to live without assistance for a while; his boys were at some risk of being spoilt, of being distanced from the realities of life.

'Money's tight,' he said. 'We're going to have to wait before we get a new one.' Jed shook his head, openly sulking. Jarlath got out some bacon and put a pan on the stove and the smell of rendering fat began to permeate the kitchen. He gave Jed a slice of buttered toast and it disappeared in two bites. Still a growing boy.

Two sets of heavy footsteps on the stairs announced the approach of the twins. Balar and Cyrus came in the kitchen, not big enough to block out the light, not literally, but the space immediately felt a lot smaller; their sheer bulk when they moved around together changed the force field of any room. They looked around the kitchen for a few moments, trying to work out what was happening with these unorthodox breakfast arrangements. Jed was not a genius, but the twins were slower still, painfully so at times, and Jarlath let them have as long as they needed to work it out.

'Ah, goddammit,' Balar eventually said in his deep, calm voice. 'Damn thing bust.'

'Yup,' said Jarlath. 'We'll be without for a time.'

'How long's a time?' asked Cyrus, but his father just shrugged. The twins would cope fine, was what he thought, and because of that—because they didn't actually need a replacement immediately—if they were his only two sons, he'd probably order one straight away. There were more factors at work, though, with the other two. There was more to get right. As he was thinking that, his fourth son, who could move around noiselessly, came into the room. Aaron was bright and light, the quickest of them and also, Jarlath often thought, the only one of his four children with a genuine mean streak. If Jarlath gave himself credit for his others sons' characters, by the same token he had to take a demerit or two for his oldest. Aaron went straight to the fridge, got some milk, took some cereal out of the cupboard, poured it into a bowl, sat and started eating.

'Five years? Six?' he said to his father. 'I suppose they design them that way on purpose. If they lasted longer we wouldn't need to keep buying them. It's a miracle how they always break at the worst possible moment. It's so inconvenient. I have a series of important meetings at work and there's a heap of washing to do.'

Jarlath felt more certain than ever about his strategy of not ordering an immediate replacement.

'Into each life a little rain must fall,' he said, an old saw which he knew irritated Aaron in particular. 'Finances are pinched at the moment. We'll have to make do for a while.' His eldest looked at him with his level grey eyes, and they held each other's gaze for a moment.

'I thought the farm was having a good year,' Aaron said.

'If you worked on it, you'd know,' said Jarlath. The truth was that the farm was indeed having a good year, but he wasn't going to tell Aaron that, and the others didn't yet know enough about farming to have worked it out for themselves. Aaron said nothing and his expression gave nothing away. He got up, washed up his bowl and left it in the drying rack before bowing to the room, with clear sarcastic intent, and going back upstairs.

'Plenty more of that to do,' said Balar, who was on his third round of toast. 'What's the day got in store, Dad?'

The answer to that was work, a whole day of it. Aaron disappeared in the good car to his important job in the town. Jarlath
was out on his tractor for most of the morning, doing chores
around the periphery of the farm. Balar was attending to the
beef cows, and took Jed along with him to help, or more accurately, to train him, though Jed was sensitive about this. It was
part of his childishness, you couldn't let him see that you saw
how little he knew. Balar might not be the brightest bulb but he
was good with his younger brother in the same way that he was
good with animals, patient and intuitive. Jarlath sent Cyrus to
the arable fields to check that everything was coming along as
it should. In the afternoon Jarlath would attend to the quarterly
accounts, ahead of the bookkeeper's imminent visit, and Cyrus
would go out on the tractor.

They took breaks to eat in mid-morning, at lunchtime, and
in the middle of the afternoon. That amounted to a reminder
of how much work in the house there always was, and would
be again until they ordered a replacement. In theory the work
was shared, but everyone knew that this period of domestic toil
was their father's idea, so it was hard for him not to end up doing
more than his fair part. Sandwiches at eleven, some defrosted
soup with bread and cheese at lunchtime, tea and yesterday's
leftover cake in the afternoon. It sounded simple enough, but
the boys ate so much, simply sucked down so many calories,
that even simple food was a lot more work than a person might
think, because cooking for ten (which is what it often felt like)
is far more work than cooking for two; Jarlath knew that before
long, he would run out of soup in the freezer, bread and cake
from their respective stores, bacon and cheese and everything
else. Cyrus could help out in the kitchen and all of them could

wash and clear and stack, with various degrees of overt reluctance, but he, Jarlath, was the only one who really knew how to cook. Knowing how to shop for food was its own separate art, and it didn't take Jarlath long to realise that for the moment, that was entirely on him. On the fourth day he sent Balar and Cyrus to do the big shop and they came back having blown the weekly budget on enough processed food to fill a paddling pool. They had also—because it was on special offer—bought an outboard motor. It was hard to be angry while also trying not to laugh.

His plans to spread the load and teach lessons came to nothing. The already-prepared food had run out, and Jarlath was cooking and feeding his big hungry boys on his own and from scratch. In addition, as Jarlath found he was pointing out with increasing frequency and decreasing tolerance, the house did not clean itself. All the beds had to be made daily. The boys' rooms were chaotic, verging on impassable, if left alone for as little as thirty-six hours—even Aaron's, which Jarlath found surprising, and a sign that his eldest was less of a self-sufficient adult than he liked to pretend. The twins shared a room, by preference rather than necessity, since the farmhouse had no shortage of space, but they treated everything as interchangeable, so their space was an area of no boundaries, of things left about at random, including billhooks and spades and mechanical equipment that they had taken upstairs out of a desire to work on them or clean them or who knew what, and then just left lying around. As for Jed, his room was unequivocally a child's room, with posters of sports teams and half-naked women and the floor invisible below an ankle-deep surf of clean and unclean clothing, indiscriminately mixed. Jarlath ordered and nagged and yelled, bossed them and cajoled and at times truly lost his temper, but it had little effect.

He was Canute and the daily chaos of ordinary life was the surging tide. And all of this just to make a point; but it became less and less clear to him what that point was. If the boys had never got used to having all these things done for them, no doubt all this would be different. But the plain fact was that they had and there was no way of acting otherwise without their seeing it as an obvious didactic ruse, and resenting it accordingly.

In the end it was the washing that did it for him. Towels and sheets and shirts and underpants and trousers and sweaters and sheets again and towels again, the most boring because they were the biggest, unless the most boring thing was socks, so many socks to wash and pair, so so many—why didn't people only wear one colour and type of sock, to make life easier? Answer, because they didn't have to. But now Jarlath had to deal with socks, and he noticed. It was pure repetition, pure attrition, and although he was now getting the boys to the point where they would throw their things into the laundry basket, and carry the basket downstairs when it was full (daily, more or less), and chuck the clothes in the washing machine after checking for colours that run, and take them out of the washing machine, and put them on the line if it was dry, though Jarlath soon abandoned that and went straight to the dryer, and take them out of the dryer, fold them, put them in a different basket and take them back upstairs and re-sort them and return them to their mandated owner—the boys being outraged if, say, Aaron ended up with Jed's socks or vice versa—the boys could only be individually persuaded to one of these tasks at a time, it was on a case-by-case basis, and every time involved a contest of wills. It was that which decided the matter. With a sense of defeat, of

making one of the inglorious strategic retreats of midlife, Jarlath
decided to cut his losses.

He began to look through the catalogues, which he had
ordered the very day the old equipment broke down. Looking back, perhaps that was a sign that he had always been more
ambivalent about the experiment than he liked to admit. There
were three main companies which made the devices, and as
usual with all such things there was a deliberate and overwhelming variety of choice. Many of the changes were small techno-
logical improvements that seemed to fill needs that no one had
ever felt, or offered nothing but the introduction of complexity
and additional features for their own sake. None of the new
stuff spoke to him of anything he actually wanted. He would
be perfectly happy ordering the same again but with better battery life and a ten-year guarantee—but that, of course, wasn't an
available option (it never was, it never is, it never will be). One
or two of the very high-end models were appealing, almost by
accident, because if you added enough features you would eventually come up with some which some possible person might
actually want: not just running baths but running them to a
prescribed temperature, not just doing the cooking and laundry,
but coordinating the tasks with a calendar so that it knew when
guests were due and therefore more or different food would be
needed, beds made to a different rota, and so on. Not that they
ever had any guests, they weren't those kind of people, that kind
of family. But if Jarlath had more help with the work, maybe
they could become those kind of people? Well—maybe. Jarlath
suspected that part of the attraction was simply in the idea of
ignoring all the practicalities and budget and ordering The Best.
In the end he did what he did last time, and ordered the cheapest

self-assembly model from the same company he'd used before. His thought was that this would involve the minimum amount of getting used to anything new.

Supper was late that night because they had to wait for Aaron to get back from town. Jarlath made a big tureen of potato soup for what he hoped was the last time in a long while. He put a chicken in the oven and mixed some flour and water and yeast to bake bread. He peeled some apples and put them on to cook over low heat. He collected the clothes baskets and put on an enormous wash, took the sheets out of the dryer and changed the beds, swept the kitchen and vacuumed the downstairs, all of this feeling so much more tiring now that he had accepted none of it was necessary and it would be coming to an end soon. Aaron got home and went up to his room and then came back down when his father called him to the table. Jarlath ladelled out the soup, cut the bread and passed it around, and watched his sons slather it with their good farm butter.

'I've got some news,' he said. 'I've ordered a replacement. It'll come tomorrow.'

Balar and Cyrus nodded. Aaron smirked. Jed looked as if he was thinking hard. They ate their soup, had seconds, then Jarlath brought over the chicken and cut it up and served it. They didn't talk much, they never did at mealtimes. When they had finished the chicken Jarlath brought over the stewed apples and brought over some cream and brown sugar and let them help themselves. Jed had been thinking all this time.

'I'd like to do the assembly,' he said. Jarlath's first impulse was to say, No, you can't—meaning not, No, you are forbidden, but, No, you are not competent to perform the task. But this would be a crushing thing to say to his youngest, especially since his brothers were looking sidelong at each other and hiding smiles. They clearly also thought that Jed couldn't manage it. He was a man, though, now, technically anyway, and sometimes the best way to learn what you can do is to try and to fail. He would be unlikely to break the device or do anything irrecoverable. Jarlath would keep an eye on him to ensure that. Besides, his older three were obviously expecting him to say no, to make sure Jed stayed the baby of the family, and it would do no harm to surprise them.

'Fine,' Jarlath said. 'If that's what you want.'

Jed looked pleased and a little startled. He had been braced to come up with arguments for why he should be given the chance. He even blushed.

'You lot can tidy up,' said Jarlath. He got up and stretched and went out onto the porch, into the evening dark. He could see as far as the lantern cast its light, just out to the picket fence, but he knew that beyond that were the fruit trees, and beyond that his land, as far as the hill in the middle distance. By day, this was his favourite view. Everything he could see belonged to him and in time would belong to his sons. Jarlath yawned, rolled his shoulders, patted his stomach, and went back inside to go upstairs and get ready for bed.

➤

The delivery came early in the morning, not long after Jarlath had begun his day. He was amused to see Jed up early too; his youngest son was excited and trying to hide it. The kit came in a crate and took two men to unload. Jed wanted to start straight away, but his father made him wait, telling him that they should have breakfast first, and that he had a couple of chores to do before he would help Jed with the unpacking. The real reason was that he didn't want Jed to be beginning on the assembly while his other sons were coming and going through the kitchen; they would be certain to make it as difficult for him as they could. That was just what brothers were like. The big box sat in the corner of the room while the young men came and went and set off about their various tasks, Balar and Cyrus on the farm as usual and Aaron heading off to his job in town.

Jarlath helped Jed take the components out of the box and made him double-check that all the parts were there, then made him go and get the necessary tools, then sat and watched while his son read through the instructions twice, start to finish. Life lessons, he thought. Then he made Jed plug in the power unit so it could charge all day while he was completing the rest of the assembly. And then, not without a sense that this experiment could go wrong and that he was operating right at the limit of his trust and confidence in Jed, he left his youngest to get on with it. The process was supposed to take five hours, which in Jarlath's experience was an overestimate, but he told his son to expect it to take up to eight.

'Take your time. Measure twice, cut once,' he told Jed.

After that he went to do office work and then a circuit round the farm. He looked in on Jed every hour or so, trying not to seem obvious about it, trying not to hover over him, and all the time wondering whether he had made the right decision. But the truth was, Jed seemed to be managing perfectly well. He was getting on slowly and methodically with the work of

assembly. Jarlath was impressed. By lunchtime, when Balar and
Cyrus came in to finish last night's soup and bread and eat half
a pound of cheese each, the top half of the unit had been completed and the battery was more than fifty per cent charged. It
looked sure that Jed would get the work finished by the end of
the day. Jarlath was pleased with the confidence he'd shown in
Jed; or rather, he was pleased that his lack of confidence had
stayed secret and hadn't been confirmed by events.

He spent the afternoon with the twins, moving the cows
between two of the top fields and attending to some problems
with their hooves. He was out for a few hours. That was a mistake. When they got back to the house, Jed had all but finished.
Or at least, he thought he had, but he had made a mistake,
an elementary and immediately obvious mistake, on the lower
half of the assembly. It was clear that he hadn't noticed and had
pressed on and, as per the instructions, had built the two halves
and then put them together and was now baffled as to why the
unit wasn't working. It was assembled and dressed and ready for
operation, but it wasn't working.

The awful thing was that the quickest, most casual glimpse
showed the problem. Jed had been so immersed in the work
that he just couldn't see what he'd done. The units were supposed to be either all-on or all-off, either working or powered
down. This model wasn't like that, however, and it stood there
blinking, smiling benignly but blankly, neither working nor
broken. Jarlath had to admit, it was very funny. This was the
worst possible moment for Aaron to come through the door; so
of course that was what happened. He came into the kitchen,
threw the good-car keys into the bowl, and, looking at the new

unit and his brother, immediately saw what had happened. The twins were looking at their own feet, snorting with the effort of suppressing laughter.

'Impossible to see what the problem is,' said Aaron in a serious voice, at which point the twins lost it. Even Jarlath, to his shame, couldn't keep in a laugh. Because the truth was, any fool could see Jed had put the unit's feet on the wrong way around. They were facing backwards. It looked ridiculous with the top and bottom half facing one way and the feet facing the other. Jed wasn't just red with embarrassment, but purple; he looked furious and he also looked as if he might be about to burst into tears. Jarlath wanted very deeply to help his youngest but knew that any sign or gesture would deepen the humiliation. He tried to project an air of assurance and comfort that he didn't feel. Jed, he was thinking, you really are a silly little boy. Look! Look, it's right in front of you!

Finally Jed saw it. He swore, and then, to his infinite credit, he laughed. He shook his head.

'Be some time before I stop hearing about this, I expect,' he said. He powered down the unit (which was still smiling, still blinking), picked up an electric screwdriver, and in ninety seconds had reattached the feet, this time the right way around. He looked at his brothers and at his father.

'Do the honours, Jed, you earned it,' said Jarlath, feeling, with one of those roller-coaster surges of emotion that parents experience, a sudden welling of pride. Because the fact was that Jed had indeed done it, and on his own. Jed powered up the unit, and in less than a minute it shifted its balance from foot to foot in an entirely human way. It was up and running.

'Hello,' said the unit, blonde, about five-foot-seven, in appearance ten years younger than Jarlath, dressed for the kitchen, eager to please, hungry for work. It was here, it was ready. You got what you paid for. From experience it would last six or seven years. Jarlath looked at his youngest and nodded.

'Hello, Mum,' said Jed.

# CHARITY

I t was my turn to open up the shop that morning, one of those cold late March days when winter stretches out its fingers from the grave with a last desperate clutch at the ankles of the escaping year. The sky was a consistent icy grey and I could feel the threat of sleet. The door handle was cold to the touch; condensation streaked the windows. I turned on the lights and the heating, put on the kettle, checked the messages, and only then went to look at the previous day's donations. There were a few items of clothing, which I put to one side. A few paperback thrillers and as so often a couple of TV chefs' cookbooks. Not much. I turned the sign at the front of the shop so that 'Closed' was on the inside, made a cup of tea and was beginning to sort through the bits and pieces when the door jangled open.

It doesn't take long to learn the categories of charity shop visitors. Donors are older, shoppers younger. Donors are divided into declutterers and the recently bereaved. The person who came through the door was a grey-haired woman in late middle age, not much younger than I am myself, struggling with a big cardboard box. Recently bereaved, I thought—declutterers tend to be more organised; the grieving are more chaotic, more emotional, more likely to be unburdening themselves metaphorically as well as literally. They require gentler handling. This woman looked like that person. I rushed around the counter to help her and between us we got her burden safely to the counter. She nodded thanks, slightly out of puff, and went back out of the shop again. Two minutes later she came back in, again struggling with a large object, this time a framed picture in brown paper wrapping.

'These were my husband's,' she said. 'Will you take them?'

'Of course,' I said. Our policy, set by the charity and enforced by my boss Winifred, is if asked, always say yes. I offered her a cup of tea and could see that she was tempted but she said no. I felt a twinge of relief—a conversation would have led to an unburdening, and I wasn't really in the mood for being unburdened upon. I already knew the gist: her husband had died. We made small talk about the weather for a few moments. She was moving more slowly as she left the shop, lingering slightly at the door; this moment of leaving behind his belongings was one more tiny goodbye. I remember thinking that I would never see her again.

I turned my attention, with no great lifting of the spirits, to the things she had left behind. The cardboard box was taped closed. I would attend to that later. I began with the main item, and untied the string around the picture. The paper slid off. At first sight it seemed to be a print, but I saw on closer inspection that it was the framed photograph of a painting—a five-foot by three-foot photograph of a hideous nineteenth century picture. The central figure was a tall fat man in uniform, not a military uniform but one of the complex colonial uniforms of a company officer or a senior customs official or something of that kind, with gilt braid, indeed frogging, on the shoulders and down the front beside the parallel rows of double-breasted buttons. He stood amid a pile of loot and a small crowd of African admirers. The general tone was of self-confidence to the point of arrogance, lavishly seasoned with pomposity and self-regard.

Well! I found it hard to imagine anyone wanting to buy the picture, except perhaps for the frame. If I had had a chance to take a good look at it, and if the circumstances around the donation had been different, I might well have turned it down. Still, you never knew. Half of the time people bought things from the shop I had to struggle against my own amazement. I put a sticker on the picture asking for £30. We would leave it at that price for a couple of weeks and then drop it in increments and if it were still the case that nobody wanted it we could always just chuck the thing away.

The day settled into its typical charity-shop pattern of lulls and flurries. At about half past eleven I found myself sorting through some miscellaneous non-antiques while a young woman, disheveled but purposeful, flicked along the clothes rail, on the hunt for bargains.

I knew her face but not her name. Once, not long before I was nudged into retirement by my 'scare,' my 'incident,' my thing-they-didn't-call-a-heart-attack-even-though-in-laymen's-terms-that's-what-it-was, I worked out how many pupils had passed through my hands during my career as a teacher. I've now forgotten the exact number. But the rough sums must have gone like this: Five classes a year of thirty each, times thirty-five years was, once I'd allowed for the fact that some of them were counted twice, more than five thousand. Then with fifteen years as a deputy head, a new intake of a hundred children a year, that's another fifteen hundred. Getting on for seven thousand children. I know that I have colleagues who remember all of them, everyone they've taught, everyone they've supervised, encouraged, told off, been laughed at by, been cheered by, been depressed by, every fine detail of every type of pupil, bright and dull, lively and deathly, most-likely-to and least-likely-to and most improved and least improved and every shade of promising-unpromising, good-bad, happy-sad, in between. I don't, though. Remember them all. My memory for faces is weak, and also my will-to-remember is not strong, at least not when it comes to my former pupils. I wish them well, of course. But things move on. They passed through my life, I passed through theirs—and now we are all, as the Americans say, in a different place.

They remember me, though, on the whole. I don't flatter myself that this is because I'm especially memorable, but simply because that is the dynamic between teachers and children. We tend to remember those who have had power over us. I can tell straight away when a former pupil comes into the shop; can tell by the not-quite-double-take they do, by the extra rigidity of their body language, or its sudden feigned casualness. Sometimes they nod and say hello. I even occasionally get a 'Hello, sir' (almost always followed by or accompanied by a blush). They are mostly girls. A specific demographic of girl, in fact, fashion-conscious and canny, because charity shops on the border of affluent metropolitan areas are famous for being a source of bargains. There are more likely to be clothes bargains when I am in the shop, too, because if clothing items are brought in and my colleagues are away I am more likely to mis-price them than they are. The opposite is true for antiques and general bric-à-brac, so I don't feel too abashed by my lack of knowledge. I have been told the names of labels to watch out for, but I find I can't retain the information. I have had lists written out for me, but mislaid them. It doesn't seem to me to matter very much. Any money brought in from the sale of donations is free money, from the charity's point of view, so I don't think it matters hugely if some former pupil or other gets an occasional bargain.

Perhaps this is only a sign that I don't care, or don't care as much as I should. That might be a fair criticism. The charity shop job is only a part-time, part-brain thing for me. I was encouraged into it by Marian, who said she thought my being at home all the time after my 'incident' and retirement was bad for me, was making me bored and grumpy. I was touched by her concern, and pleased that she still minded enough about my moods to notice them and want to affect them. It took me a little while to realise that what she really minded was having me 'underfoot'—her word, used over the phone when she didn't know that I could overhear. Well, on reflection, of course that was what it was. She had had the house to herself all day in term time for more than a third of a century. She had her friends and her interests and her life and her typical day, which was entirely hers to fill. A moping, shuffling husband, requiring, if not to be entertained, then at least to be occasionally interacted with, was not part of the marital arrangement, as Marian had come to understand it. So she suggested that I look for something just interesting enough to keep me out of the house, but not sufficiently demanding to be mentally stressful or physically taxing.

Perhaps I have held back a degree of commitment from the work because I resent this underlying dynamic: it's not a real job, it's merely something to stop me from annoying my wife. Back in dim antiquity, when I was training as a teacher, we used to be told that all true learning is goal-directed. Perhaps all work is goal-directed too. But it's hard to feel that selling old scarves and mirrors and Clive Cussler paperbacks is an activity deeply charged with meaning, even if the proceeds do go to fund research on MS.

Now I turned my attention to a to-do list left by Winifred, the shop manager, who despite her name—or perhaps, if one took a sufficiently broad view of changing fashions in upper-middle-class nomenclature, because of it—was a young woman in her late twenties. She was proud of her name and of its flexibility, and would happily go by the full version (which is what I called her), Winny, Win, Fred, or, her own favourite among her contemporaries, Wizz. Winifred was the shop's secret weapon. She could and perhaps should have been running something bigger and more demanding, but she had lost a beloved uncle to MS over the course of her teenage years and was genuinely committed to raising money for the charity. It was her interest in clothes and eye for them which brought so many good things to the shop. Well-off people donating things to charity much prefer it when the person accepting the donation understands and appreciates the thing being donated. It was Winifred who would write out lists of names for me to watch out for, and I often suspected that at least some of them were in-jokes and teases, since it was hard to believe that anyone would spend hundreds of pounds on anything made by anyone called Bathing Ape, A Child of the Jago, Off-White or Been Trill. Still, if these were jokes at my expense, I didn't mind them, since Winifred was such a pleasant person to work with. I must also admit that there was a tiny sub-erotic twang in the fact that my boss was an attractive woman three and a half decades younger than I. It combined very agreeably with the fact that I had no responsibilities at all.

The note read: 'Mr P, nothing special on today but remember we have to start in on the annual accounts soon. So just do the drop-offs. W x'

Her wish, my command. The main drop-off was the widow's cardboard box. It was rectangular, longer than it was wide, say four feet by two. I felt the melancholy I always have at a posthumous donation, the sad process by which the things which have meaning for us as individuals gradually leak it away after our deaths and become anonymous, contextless, meaningless stuff. Almost everything which passes through our hands in the charity shop was loved by somebody once, whatever it was— coat or skirt or earring or vinyl record or book or brooch or necklace or shoes or picture or photo-frame or hat or scarf or set of plates—these things were all once loved. But then the person who loved them either stopped feeling the same about them, or died. It is the undercurrent to our work in the shop, loss of feeling, loss and grief. When people come and buy these bits and pieces, we're hoping that meaning will be restored to them—that they will once again mean something to somebody. That their spirits, their anima, will be restored to them.

Even if I had not known, I would have been able to guess that this was a donation in the aftermath of somebody's death: the objects had a coherence and a belonging-to-someoneness, not the sense of random accumulation and discard you get from a spring clear-out. A leather portfolio for papers, streaked with age; a beautiful unused pipe, gleaming with dark light, and a set of cleaners to go with it; a hip flask made out of what looked like but surely could not be silver; an ivory-coloured stick with some sort of attachment on the end; a set of four heavy crystal tumblers, wrapped in old broadsheet newspaper; nine beer mats decorated with drawings of vintage cars; a pair of folding binoculars in a heavy wood and leather case. A man's belongings, things which had once had meaning and purpose for him, and now, after his death, were nothing but bits and pieces of soulless matter.

While I was sorting through the box, the girl who had been rummaging through the clothing rail came over to the desk and watched what I was doing. I say 'girl'—she would have left school but not for long and would barely be twenty. From her body language I could tell she was a former pupil.

'You're from St Michael's,' I said. This is the formula I have developed to show that I know that pupils recognise me, while being noncommittal on the issue of whether or not I remember them. She nodded, pleased.

'Alice Marshall. I was in your English class. 5D. We did *Of Mice and Men*.'

'Of course we did,' I said, my voice not carrying the heavy ironic burden which might have been appropriate. I taught that book to countless numbers of children over the years and came to feel a sincere loathing for Steinbeck's platitudes. The only book I have taught more often and come to despise even more is *Lord of the Flies*. Glasses with prescriptions for short-sight cannot be used to start a fire in the manner that Piggy's spectacles are. 'How are you? What are you doing now?'

'I'm at uni. Doing fashion at St Martin's.'

'Excellent,' I said. And now that I looked more closely I could see that what had seemed dishevelment, indeed had not seemed too far from the condition of someone who had put their clothes on in the dark while wearing mittens, was on second sight more intended and designed and put-together, with a baggy outer long coat covering a cardigan which in turn covered not one but two shirts, and below that a complicated skirt which had tears and rips that I knew, because Winifred had told me, were there on purpose. She was carrying an enormous handbag decorated in patchwork. I had learnt that clothing items which were torn, holed, asymmetrical, and mis-matching were indicators of potential value. Of course they could also mean that the items in question were torn, holed, asymmetrical and mismatching; there were no guarantees. That was why I needed Winifred. On the other hand, when it came to things like the freshly donated miscellanea in this box on the counter, she needed me, too. It is pleasant, and rare enough, to be needed just enough to feel the fact, but to have no concomitant obligations.

Alice was looking down at the box and its contents.

'Go ahead,' I said. 'Help yourself.'

She picked up the leather portfolio and opened it. A nicely made piece, to my eye, though not an especially convenient size, slightly too large to be carried in the same manner as a briefcase but not big enough to be utile for, say, an artistically inclined student such as Alice. I could see that she liked the used texture of the case. She put it back down and picked up the pipe and held it up to catch the light.

'Ceci n'est pas une pipe,' said Alice. She wiggled the pipe from side to side. My opinion of her shifted slightly with that reference to Magritte. The revelation about her fashion degree had made me think she was, how best to put this without seeming rude, travelling in the slow lane. I had misjudged her. She was curious, lively, I now saw. I like that in a former pupil, perhaps for reasons of displaced vanity—it makes me feel that I did a decent job. Any sign of a student having read a book I take as a personal victory. She put the pipe back down, flicked through the beer mats, and then picked up the stick.

'I have to admit that I don't know what that is,' I said.

She gave me a quick smile. 'I don't think they used to have them, er . . .' She was trying not to say 'in your day'. 'It's a selfie stick. You know, for taking selfies.'

This was half unfair and half fair. I have always kept up with technology and buy a new smartphone every couple of years. In reply to Alice, and to make this point, I took my Samsung S9 out of my pocket and held it up in front of her in silent rebuke. However, it is also true that I have never taken a selfie.

'I like it,' she said. 'Can I have a go?'

I nodded. Alice took her phone out of her huge bag and clipped it into the end of the selfie stick. Then, sucking in her cheeks, she held it out in front of her and took a photo.

'Wow!' she said. 'Great! Magic! Best selfie I ever took. How much for the selfie stick, Mr Potter?'

I held out my hands and took the stick from her. At first touch, I could tell there was something wrong with it. The material was a stained, streaky off-yellow, not ivory but something not far removed from it, probably some other kind of bone. The bracket on the end of the stick, the place where the phone should go, was made out of a different, darker material. The little stick felt much too heavy for its size and appearance—

as if a heavier object had been crammed into the form of this smaller one. The temperature was wrong too: the stick had the look of a cold thing but was blood-warm to the touch. My instinct, suddenly, coming from a hunch that I couldn't explain, was to tell her that it wasn't for sale. But that would make no sense. We were a charity shop and selling things was what we did. I shook off the misgiving.

'For a former pupil, five pounds,' I said. I would have put it on sale for twenty pounds, or sold it to a friend for ten pounds, so this seemed to me a very good deal. Alice clearly agreed, and got the money out of her purse with alacrity. I asked if she was in employment, as well as at college, and it turned out that she had a part-time job at a hairdresser, so I got her to fill out a Gift Aid form. She left the shop with the top of the stick protruding from her handbag. I went through the rest of the contents of the box, labelling the bits and pieces with price stickers; the beer mats I put to one side for a Google check, just to make sure that they weren't some sort of collector's item (they weren't—but with anything that looks like a full set of something, I've learnt that it is worth taking the trouble to be sure).

It was eight weeks before I saw Alice again. I had been thinking about her, though, because for some reason, the box and the portfolio and the beer mats and the stick stayed with me. I found myself wondering who it was had died, and of what, and what the history of the objects had been. There was something about the feel of the stick that stayed with me too. I had a series of dreams about objects being the wrong temperature: about a roast chicken which I took out of the oven and carried over to the dinner table and cut up and tasted only to find it ice-cold, inedible; about picking up a cup of cold water and it turning to boiling hot tea as it began to go down my throat—a dream from which I woke choking, gasping, with a racing heart. I dreamt about a skeleton on fire, in the corner of my GP's surgery, standing there with flames dancing all over its bones while everybody pretended not to notice and ignored me when I tried to shout a warning—again, I woke directly from that dream, shouting incoherently, Marian beside me shaking my shoulder, half-worried, half-annoyed.

Work went past in its ordinary manner. The picture of the African colonialist was still unsold and still on the wall behind the counter. Through April and May Winifred was in the throes of what I knew to be (unofficially, since it was not discussed in front of her) a bad break-up and as a result was distracted and not quite herself. Around the end of June, with the weather now hot, I was working at the counter of the shop—or rather, sitting behind it doing the crossword, since donations had been slow and there was nothing to sort through and, as a result, next to nothing to do. Three young women came in, a typical crew of fashionistas on the lookout for bargains. I knew from Winifred that we didn't have much new stuff of interest and had half a mind to tell them so. They were scantily clad from the heat, in the new London manner whereby warm weather causes people to dress for Copacabana Beach. The girls split up and started tackling separate rails of clothes. They had given me a look as they came in, so I knew they were former pupils. They muttered among themselves and passed items backwards and forwards and then after about twenty minutes advanced towards the till in a V formation, one in front and the other two behind. The one taking the lead was a very skinny girl with bright eyes.

'Mr Potter?' she said. I have already admitted that faces are not my great strength, and was about to make my standard were-you-at St-Michael's speech, then I realised with a shock that I did in fact recognise her. It was Alice. But she looked completely different, so much thinner that all her features had fundamentally transformed. Her eyes were so much bigger they were like the eyes on a cartoon; her head was bigger in proportion to her body, her entire physique had changed. She was wearing a light shift dress and a light outer layer on top covering it, and it was only when she moved that I could see how shockingly thin she had become.

'Alice,' I said. 'Nice to see you again. Anything I can do for you?'

The other two girls had chosen pieces off the rail, and held them out to me. I think they were embarrassed to have a former teacher serving them in a shop; it was not the first time I had encountered that reaction. I made small talk to help the moment pass, but while I was doing so I was consumed by the transformation in Alice. She was at that stage of emaciation where the skin seems almost transparent and the flesh is barely covering the bones beneath; it was as if she were a skeleton with the merest cosmetic layer concealing it. Her outer shell was as light as paper. I could see a tiny layer of fuzz, like the outer surface of a peach, on her face. I took the money from her friends and put their chosen items (a leather skirt, a T-shirt of the sort that was torn on purpose) into a bag with the charity's logo on it, but as I did so all I could think of was what had happened to Alice.

'Are you well?' I eventually said. She nodded, without making eye contact. She seemed shy and proud at the same time.

'I'm doing my end-of-year project. It's about selfies and self-image. That stick you sold me has come in really handy. I use it all the time.'

One of the girls had a reaction to that, I saw—she looked first at her friend and then at me and then at Alice.

'There's just something about it,' she said. 'The pictures just come out differently from any other pictures. Better. It's like it knows how I want to look. That sounds silly. But anyway,' she trailed off, blushing and mumbling, 'the tutor likes the project.'

'I'm glad to hear that and I'm glad to see you, Alice,' I said. The girl who had glanced across was looking at me meaningfully, as if trying to convey a message. Her affect was worried or angry, but more than that I couldn't say. The three of them left the shop, the doorbell jangling in their wake and my nerves jangling too, for some reason I couldn't explain. I went to the door and looked out into the street to watch Alice and her friends walking away. I had an uneasy sense that there was something I should have said or done; something I should have noticed but had missed.

I turned and went back into the shop. The first thing I saw was the picture that had been brought in on the same day I met Alice. The pompous man in his uniform with his loot around him and the grateful procession of natives behind. He was sneering, or smiling, it was difficult to tell. A cold face, an arrogant face, a face whose owner was good at putting himself first. As I stood looking, the door jangled open and one of the girls who'd been shopping with Alice came bursting into the shop. She was looking over her shoulder as she came in and then came over to the counter and, most unexpectedly, grabbed me by the arm.

'She's sick,' said the girl. She was gasping, with anxiety or suppressed tears or from the sprint back to the shop. 'Alice. You have to do something. She won't listen to us.' She took her phone out of her pocket and held it up. 'I pretended to leave this as an excuse.' She turned and went to the door again. 'Please do something.' And then she was gone.

I thought I knew what she meant, but had no idea what to do. I came out of the shop, but she was already out of sight; she must have run around the corner after Alice and her other friend. I went back inside; I felt anxious and helpless. The portrait behind the counter seemed to be sneering down at me. It was not a case that 'the eyes follow you around the room,' it was the opposite. The fixity and rigidity of his expression, his oblivious and unchanging self-love, seemed impervious to any reaction. This man would never care what anyone thought or did. His eyes would never follow you anywhere. As far as he was concerned, you did not exist. I was suddenly full of a wish to know more about him, who he was and where the painting was made and what the story behind the painting had been. But I had no details for the woman, the widow, who had brought it to the shop. I had thought I would never see her again. Unless . . .

I went over to the painting and with some difficulty turned it over. And there it was, as if at an auction room, a sticker with the owner's name and address: I recognised it as one of the big nineteenth century houses a street or two away. My impulse was to drop everything and go there immediately, but I felt that would be letting Winifred down—also, just as importantly, she might be dropping in that afternoon, and I didn't want to be caught in a dereliction of duty.

It was the right call. Winifred did indeed come, not more than a half an hour later, saying that she needed to check that the accounts were in order. She had moved past the sad, distracted phase of her break-up to a mode in which she was busy, pragmatic, on with the next thing. I asked her to cover for me while I popped out for a moment, and she agreed, carefully not seeming curious.

The house was an end-of-terrace late Victorian building with net curtains and a large bronze door knocker. I knocked and waited. No one came to the door and for a moment I felt relief. I had got involved in something that wasn't my business and if there was nothing practical I could do, then I had tried and failed and I could let the matter rest. To make sure my conscience was clear, I knocked again, and this time could hear approaching footsteps. The door opened and I was met by the grey-haired woman who had come into the charity shop those several weeks before. I could tell she didn't know who I was. She didn't say anything: she was used to people coming to the door trying to sell things.

'Um,' I said, realising that I should have prepared what I was going to say, but hadn't. 'This is awkward.'

'How so?' she asked. I don't think she had been expecting the caller to be a well-spoken man of my age.

'I work at the charity shop,' I said. 'The one where you made a generous donation a few weeks ago. A painting and a box. It's just, well, it's hard to explain,' I said, trailing off.

She gave me a long, assessing look. Then she opened the door more widely.

'You'd better come in,' she said. I followed her through a tidy hallway into the kind of sitting room all these houses have, with bay windows and sofas and books, but with one startling feature: the real-life original of the painting whose photo she had given to us. At this full-size, the man's face gleamed with avidity, with appetites slaked and unslaked. I had a sudden thought: the painter had really hated this man.

She must have seen me do a double-take.

'My late husband's ancestor. His evil ancestor, as it turns out.'

'I'd love to hear the story,' I said.

'Tea?' she said. I said yes. She went away into her kitchen. I took the chance to get up and take a long look at the painting. I was already familiar with the main subject. Beside the man were two tables covered in loot: a gold box spilled jewels; a set of plates and saucers looked as if they might be solid silver. In the background there was a half-African, half-Tuscan palace, and in the middle distance a group of half-naked Africans could be seen approaching in a train or procession; the atmosphere was reverential, supplicatory. He was a powerful man being asked for a favour, and offered tribute, by grateful indigenes. On looking more closely, I could see that the train of grateful people were carrying at the front of their procession a picture or icon which, if you looked nearly at it, you could see was the same as this very painting. Perhaps, if you got out a magnifying glass, you could see again that the smaller version of the painting at the front of the procession had on it another, even smaller version. The implication was clear: the grateful locals did not just love their lord and master, they revered him—perhaps, even, to the point of worship. It was an uncomfortable thing to look at and I was glad when my hostess returned with a tea tray and sat with a straight back across from me on the sofa.

'Robert grew interested in family history as he got older. By no means an unusual pastime. He was a solicitor, so he was always good with paper, with tracking things down. It took up more and more of his time. He retired a few years ago and, well, didn't exactly become a full-time genealogist, but not far off.'

'Good to have a hobby,' I said, thinking of how irritated Marian had been by having me permanently underfoot. From her face, I could tell that she thought that was a stupid thing to say.

'Robert's family were Belgian. They lived in the Congo. He liked that, especially as he was the sort of person who never went anywhere himself. He became particularly interested in . . .' She gestured at the picture. It was as if she did not want to say the man's name. 'An ancestor, great-great-grand-uncle or something like that. From that imperial generation. He made the family rich, for a generation or two at least. They lost all the money doing stupid things with investments, but this man'—again she pointed, again she did not name him—'was always spoken of as a great person. About the only trace of him that was left was that painting, which somehow came down to Robert, maybe because nobody else wanted it. Anyway, after years of these researches, and very much out of character, Robert decided that he wanted to go and see the place where the ancestor lived. The place in that painting. In the Democratic Republic of Congo. He asked me to go with him but we decided we couldn't afford it for both of us. Also, frankly, I just didn't want to. Robert was gone for two weeks and when he got back he was different. He stopped talking about genealogy but he wouldn't say why. Then one night he got a bit tipsy and said that he'd found out things he didn't like about the ancestor and that there were two sides to every story and that some of the things he had found out were dark—that was his word, dark. He said that he had found out about horrors and about crimes and about greed. He said that his ancestor had been guilty of atrocities. The house, the

palace, where he lived had been razed, he said—burnt down, on
purpose, by the locals. And then he never spoke about it, ever
again, after that one night. He kept the picture up, though. He
loved it despite what he knew.'

She paused and picked up her cup and then put it back down
without having drunk from it.

'And he was not the same person after that. It was as if he
went into himself. He was a talkative man, Robert, a man
who liked to share his enthusiasms. He could'—she smiled—
'he could go on a bit. But after he got back from the Congo
he talked much less. He took photographs all the time instead.
He had this stick for taking pictures, that he'd bought in the
place where his ancestor lived. It was the only memento he'd
found. He bought it from a man in the grounds of the place
where that'—the picture, again—'place used to stand. Robert
thought it was funny, bringing this thing back. But it was as if
he became obsessed with it and with his own image. He just
kept taking photos. And he said he liked the way he looked, it
was as if suddenly and out of the blue he had become incredibly vain of his appearance. But it was mad, because at the same
time he stopped taking any care about what he ate and drank
and he was getting fatter and fatter, and that was a very bad
thing for him because of his blood pressure and cholesterol and
everything else. But he kept saying, I look great, I can see the
evidence. Vainer and fatter and iller all at once. And then he
had a massive heart attack, right here in this room, with that
bloody thing in his hand, taking one last picture, and he died.'

I didn't know what to say, so I didn't say anything. It was a
sad story and I should have felt sad, but what I felt instead was a
growing sense of physical distaste, a crawling sensation whose

source I could not locate. I made reassuring noises, which I know did nothing to reassure, and said words designed to comfort which I know did nothing to comfort, and I left to go back to the shop. As I walked I had one thought: Alice. This man's death had something to do with Alice. More, it had something to do with the object he had brought back from his travels. It was incomprehensible but I was sure it was true.

'What's the matter?' said Winifred as soon as I came through the door. I thought to stall and deflect, but then thought there was no point—she could tell I was worried. So I told her the story, from the beginning, and to my grateful relief she took it seriously. After I finished she sat, nodding slowly. Then she gave one final brisk nod as she made up her mind.

'Let's go get it back,' she said.

'Get what back?'

'The stick. We'll get it back, return her money, and chuck it away. It's—well, I don't want to say.'

'Gift Aid,' I said. Winifred knew what I meant. We went to the filing cabinet and went through the last couple of months' paperwork. I found the form with Alice's address on it. We closed and locked the shop and walked the fifteen minutes to the modern block of flats where Alice lived. I rang the bell, a girl's voice answered, we said we were there for Alice and she said 'second floor' and buzzed us in. I was a little out of breath by the time I got to the flat, where the door had been left ajar.

We went in and to my surprise Alice's friend, the one who had told me to do something, was waiting for us. She understood my look.

'I don't live here. Her mum doesn't want to leave her alone when she's like this and she has to go to work so I'm sort of babysitting. She's in bed.' She said nothing about the fact that I had been worried enough to act on her worry; to her it evidently seemed natural.

'We've come for the selfie stick,' said Winifred. The friend looked at her and then at me and we looked back.

'She has it with her,' she said. 'She always has it with her.'

'Then we'll have to go in and take it,' I said.

'I don't think Alice would like that very much,' she said, but tentatively. 'I'll go in first.'

She went down the corridor and was gone for about five minutes. Winifred and I stayed standing and didn't speak. The main room of the flat had modern furniture and large black-and-white photographs on the walls, and had a busy person's orderliness. Alice's friend came back.

'You can go in,' she said. She led us down the hall and showed us through the doorway and then came in behind us.

Alice's room was decorated with a (presumably ironic) boy-band poster and two Cartier-Bresson photographs, but it had the psychic aroma of a sick person's space. She was propped up in bed against pillows. Her eyes were huge and her clavicles were cutting through the cloth of her T-shirt. Next to her on the coverlet were a fashion magazine, her phone and the selfie stick. She seemed anxious but it was also as if she had been waiting for us.

'Mr Potter,' she said.

'Alice, this is Winifred, who runs the shop. We've come'—and I had a sudden moment of inspiration, because my intention had been to demand the stick back, to tell Alice that we were going to take it from her irrespective of what she wanted, but I realised that would be an act of emotional violence, might well do her harm in itself, so I heard myself saying—'because the original owner wants that thing back. Her sister brought it in by mistake. She thought she was being helpful, but it's a precious heirloom. It has all these memories of her husband. She says she can't live without it. I'm so sorry, it's a terrible mistake, just one of those things that happens, but we do need it back.'

Alice's eyes filled with tears. Her hand made an involuntary motion towards the stick. Winifred, bless her, went straight in to help me.

'Just one of those awful things,' she said, 'we're so sorry.'

'I can't,' said Alice, very quietly. 'I can't.'

'I'm so sorry but you have to,' said Winifred, also quietly and gently, but undeflectable. Alice's friend seemed to be holding her breath.

Alice clutched the stick and rubbed her hand up and down it, up and down, slowly. Then she pushed it across the coverlet and turned her face to one side. Alice's friend came past us and picked it up and then, holding it at arm's length, dropped it into my hands. I instantly felt the same sense of unease that I had the last time I touched the stick; the sense that the temperature and materials of the stick were all wrong, that it was made of something unnatural and malevolent.

It was clear that Alice didn't want to say anything more. We left quickly and went into the hallway of the flat.

'It'll be all right now,' I said to her friend, certain that it was true, but not knowing why. 'She's going to get better.'

The friend, who had tears in her eyes, just nodded.

'But let us know,' said Winifred. The friend nodded again. We went down to the street and Winifred pointed to a black rubbish bin across the road. We crossed to it and I dropped the stick into the bin. In the last split second before I let go of it I had a sensation that it had gone intensely cold, not just the stick itself; a stinging coldness went all the way up my left arm. Winifred puffed out her cheeks.

'Wow,' she said. 'You probably want to wash your hands and you definitely want a drink, so let's find a pub. The shop can take care of itself for the rest of today.'

'Yes and yes,' I said. We started heading back to our part of town, walking more slowly than we had come. But then I stopped.

'I have to know,' I said. Winifred grabbed my arm.

'Please don't,' she said.

'I'm sorry. I have to know. I have to see for myself.'

'Please,' she said again, and Winifred looked so aghast it made me pause for a moment. And yet the feeling that I needed to know was too strong for me. I had no choice. I squeezed Winifred's hand in what was meant to be reassurance, and took it off my arm.

'A single look, that's all,' I said. She looked so scared for me that I almost lost the strength to do what I was compelled to do.

I walked back to the rubbish bin and picked up the stick. It had gone back to feeling warm to the touch, almost blood-hot. I took my phone out of my pocket and inserted it into the clamp at the end. I plugged the connector into the headphone jack, held the phone at arm's length, and took my first-ever selfie. I took the phone out of the clamp, opened the picture up and looked at the image I had taken.

It was a photograph of me, of course. But I did not look human. The shirt and jacket and top of the chest were recognisably mine, but skin from my face had been flayed and peeled off. It was the head of a skeleton—my skeleton. My eyeballs were hanging out. Maggots were writhing all over the bones of my skull and pouring down my body. It was not a still photograph: the maggots were moving. They were crawling down my shirt and I felt sure that if I held on to the phone they would crawl out of the image and onto my arm, blood-hot, burning, itching, swollen.

Vomit rose to the back of my throat. I stepped forward and threw the stick into the bin. And then I threw the phone after it and turned my back and hurried down the street towards Winifred, who was standing with her arms folded, her face white, anxiously expectant, waiting to hear the worst.

# ACKNOWLEDGMENTS

Four of these stories have been published elsewhere, in slightly different forms and (sometimes) different titles:

"Signal" was published in *The New Yorker*.
"Coffin Liquor" and "Reality" were published in the *London Review of Books*.
"We Happy Few" was published in *Esquire*.

I am grateful to the editors of all these publications.